Rise and Walk

By

Gregory Solis

Hadrian Publishing

WWW.HADRIANPUBLISHING.COM

Rise and Walk

Copyright © 2007 Gregory Solis

All Rights Reserved. This book is a work of fiction. The characters and situations in this story are imaginary. No resemblance is intended between these characters and any real persons, either living, dead or undead.

No part of this book may be reproduced or transmitted in any form or by any means, graphic, electronic, or mechanical, including photocopying, recording, taping or by any informational storage retrieval system, without the written permission of the publisher.

Released by Hadrian Publishing.

Published through Lulu.com

3131 RDU Center

Suite210

Morrisville NC, 27560

For information E-mail

Riseandwalk@gmail.com

Cover design by Apocryphal Graphics

Photography by Christina Grill

Edited by Christina Grill and Cassie Goodwin

ISBN 978-1-4303-0600-9

Written in the United States of America

For Christina,

You have made me so very happy.

Table of contents

Chapter 1 .... Page 1
Chapter 2 .... Page 8
Chapter 3 .... Page 13
Chapter 4 .... Page 18
Chapter 5 .... Page 25
Chapter 6 .... Page 28
Chapter 7 .... Page 35
Chapter 8 .... Page 39
Chapter 9 .... Page 45
Chapter 10 .... Page 49
Chapter 11 .... Page 60
Chapter 12 .... Page 64
Chapter 13 .... Page 67
Chapter 14 .... Page 71
Chapter 15 .... Page 75
Chapter 16 .... Page 79
Chapter 17 .... Page 83
Chapter 18 .... Page 93
Chapter 19 .... Page 97
Chapter 20 .... Page 102
Chapter 21 .... Page 106

Chapter 22	Page 112
Chapter 23	Page 116
Chapter 24	Page 119
Chapter 25	Page 121
Chapter 26	Page 132
Chapter 27	Page 139
Chapter 28	Page 144
Chapter 29	Page 152
Chapter 30	Page 159
Chapter 31	Page 165
Chapter 32	Page 171
Chapter 33	Page 178
Chapter 34	Page 182
Chapter 35	Page 186
Chapter 36	Page 193
Chapter 37	Page 198
Chapter 38	Page 200
Chapter 39	Page 215
Chapter 40	Page 218

Acknowledgements

Thanks to my dear family, mother and father, my brothers Wayne and Dan for their love and support.

Special thanks to my sweet girlfriend Christy for her unending faith in me.

This book would not exist if it were not for my friends, my brother Robert, Johnny O, Joseph, Fermin, Scotty C, Peter, Jordan, Steve K, Finch, Jana, Gretchen, Zhaddi, Adam, Sanna, my old friend Cassie, my pal Tracy, and the Thrillseekers.

I have to also send out special thanks to those people whom have been a wealth of advice and encouragement over the years... Michael Trigilio, Mark Lamb, Bob Kaputof, and Nancy Malone.

Thanks to George A. Romero and company for all the fun nightmares.

My gratitude goes to those brave writers who have kept the scene alive, David Moody, Len Barnhart, Brian Keene, Bryan Smith, and of course, S.D. Perry. Thanks to S.K. for On Writing and all the dark chests of wonders.

And a special heartfelt thanks to all the Zombie fans out there.

Gregory Solis

January 1, 2007

Rise and Walk

One

Many people are afraid of the dark, but Gary Jones had good cause. In all his nineteen years he had never before experienced such terror. He fled almost blind, through the mountain forest, groping to avoid the trees. The only illumination provided by the moonless night was a faint glow of starlight fighting through the thick clouds. His leg throbbed from a bad step that he had taken while evading his pursuers. Clutched in his right hand was an aluminum sample canister, much like a small thermos. Gary held the container close to his body as he ran. He knew he must get the contents of the canister back to civilization. First he would have to avoid his classmates, who were trying to eat him.

Gary wondered how he would recount the details of his ordeal to the authorities. The police might think him a lunatic and who could blame them. No sane person would believe the horrific events that he had just witnessed. As he propelled his tired body forward he tried to keep the facts fresh in his mind to reassure himself that he was not going mad.

His summer term geology course at the Junior College had camped out for a night in the mountains to examine some exposed rock formations. As the students prepared to leave, they spoke of an excursion to the pizza parlor in town. Everyone was jovial with the thought of returning home.

The evening peace was shattered when a meteor burst through the heavy clouds with a supersonic blast. Professor Galloway, a man very excited by the prospect of scientific discovery, sent the students to search in teams.

The students located the meteorite two kilometers away in pristine condition. The Geiger counter measured no discernible radiation making it safe for recovery. The coconut sized traveler was so hot from its trip through the atmosphere that its heat deformed the shovel used to carry it back to camp. Carefully obtained scrapings were tested chemically and revealed it to be composed of olivine, a form of iron. The Professor decided to stay in the field until the meteorite cooled enough to be safely transported back to the campus.

Gary's classmates did not share the Professor's interest in interstellar discoveries. They were hungry and wanted to go home. The Professor told the students that discoveries of this nature were historic because the meteorite was most likely older than the earth. A find of this nature superseded their dinner plans. The Professor's decision did not make him a popular man. A group of impatient athletes who often taunted Gary decided to accelerate the meteorite's cooling by dousing it with cold water. The temperature differential caused the meteorite to shatter and throw a steamy dark green mist over four of their class. The spray caused chemical burns, seizure and within minutes, death.

The Professor ordered camp struck while examining the fallen students. He asked Gary to place the surviving bits of meteorite in a biohazard container. Recovering the broken meteorite was tense work but Gary was a talented student and knew the safety protocols.

Mindy, a freshmen cheerleader who wore her uniform with pride, though too often, cautioned Gary not to touch the meteorite. He was surprised at her warning. Those were the first words Mindy had ever spoken to him. He had admired her body from afar all summer, yet never caught her eye with his excellence in academia. She was in a panic trying to use her cell phone with no results. Gary remembered suggesting that she go start the bus. That was just before the screams rang out.

Clark Evens, the local baseball sensation with the eighties hair cut, was the first to awaken. The Professor was checking for a pulse, when Clark raised his head and bit the kindly scholar on his wrist. Gary remembered Professor Galloway holding his bloody arm as the blistered and burned athlete attacked once more.

He recalled his deceased classmates rising to their unsteady feet and attacking the other students. Amongst the screams, blood and confusion, Gary backed away into the darkness of the trees to watch the Professor die. He wanted to escape, but the forest was too dark. After waiting a few desperate moments he crept in fear towards the vehicle. When Gary reached the school bus he recoiled in horror at what he saw. In the drivers seat the Professor was taking large bites from the body of the once beautiful Mindy. Blood ejected out of her artery as the Professor tore at her soft neck. When Gary tried to pull the Professor off the young girl, he snapped back with blood stained teeth. The Professor growled like a wild animal as he returned to claw at Mindy's helpless body. Gary left her to be devoured, too terrified to be of any assistance. He would never forget her cries for mercy.

The guilt of leaving her would be unbearable, yet he knew that whatever was in the container was responsible for infecting the others. He tried to press himself on with the thought that he must find a way to bring the sample back to a lab for proper analysis. He hid for a few heart pounding minutes in the cover of the trees until he no longer heard screams. He saw his dead classmates in the distant light of the fire stand and wobble around like some evil newborn animals; unsure of their footing. *How could any of this happen?* He thought that the answer must lie within the fragments that he was carrying. His risen classmates began to walk, some in his direction. He sprinted into the forest, no longer afraid of the dark.

Gary was so very tired. He had been running with no point of reference to guide his course. Thoughts of resting echoed in his frightened mind but he did not dare. All he had now was running, yet injured, he was not moving very fast. He had to stop, if just for a moment. *Perhaps climb a tree and hide. But what if they find me and I become trapped in the middle of nowhere. What if they climb up after me?* He resolved that climbing a tree was not a good idea. With all of his exertion, Gary could not hear if anyone was behind him. He had to stop soon and catch his breath. *In a moment*, he thought, *just a little further.*

No longer able to endure the pain in his left shin, he felt his way behind a large tree and stopped in silence. A nightmarish moment passed as Gary strained to listen for his classmates. All he could hear was the wild pounding of his heart thumping in his head. He tried to breathe as quietly as possible but his lungs were famished. As his body calmed, he noticed the faint sounds of a stream in the distance. There were streams all over the mountain that led to Lake Sierra. *Water would be nice,* he thought as he took note of his thirst. If he could swim, the water should carry him down the mountain to someone who would help. *Swimming would be easier on my leg,* he thought. He noticed a small flicker of light in the far distance. It looked dim but he thought it might be a campfire. Gary started towards the light while trying to edge closer to the sound of the stream.

He walked with determination to keep his aching body moving when mind shattering fear sprang upon him. Gary heard a deep, dry, raspy throated exhalation of air from his right. Someone or something was next to him. Cold sweat beaded on his brow as Gary felt his stomach tense into rigid knots. He smelled uncooked meat and perfume as something tackled his right side. Gary's left leg buckled under the attack. Disoriented in the darkness, the hard ground hit him sooner than he expected. Long fingernails scratched at his face. He felt the terrible sting of teeth in his shoulder. Through fabric, skin, and the meat of Gary's arm, he felt his attacker bite down so hard that one of the monster's teeth broke on his bone. Horrid growls and the gnashing of braces snapped in the air. Gary grabbed at his attacker and felt that it was a she, wearing a skirt. He cast her off with what was left of his strength and realized that his assailant was Mindy, the cheerleader. He got to his feet and sprinted towards the sound of the stream. He felt his shoulder, bloody and bitten. Through the intense pain, Gary discovered an overwhelming desire to live. He was bleeding but not gushing out blood; his arteries must be okay. If he could get to the water he could have a chance. He heard rustling noises in the darkness. *There are more of them!* Gary realized that the light he saw, the campfire, was actually his camp. He had unknowingly run in a large circle. His disappointment turned to anger. Directly in his path were two of his former classmates. He was determined to go right through them and get to the stream.

The world had to know what was in the meteorite and find a way to prevent this from happening to anyone else. Gary felt hands grasping for him as he made his way past a deep groan. In the darkness, he dodged another hellish wail. Gary felt the earth come out from underneath his feet as he plummeted into a rushing stream. Ice cold water enveloped him for a frozen moment until he broke the surface gulping for air. He picked up speed in the frigid drift as the current pulled him along. He held on tight to the canister with his right hand while using his left to swim. His right arm was useless for rotation due to his bite wound but he could still hold on to the sample. He grew very tired and began to forget about the pain. The biting chill made him sleepy yet he had to stay awake. He had to find someone and explain what he had witnessed. He struggled to maintain consciousness as the water drove him faster downstream. He thought of his parents and family. He thought of Mindy with the great ass and how he did not want to die a virgin. The frigid mountain stream was starting to bite at his body as he grew numb with hypothermia. The pain in his shoulder drummed to the beat of his failing heart. Slower and slower, but he had to stay alive. He faded in his efforts; his consciousness dissolving in and out as the current pulled him forward.

    The stream opened up into a large body of water. His pace slowed and Gary could see the waning glow of campfires some distance down the shore. He struggled with stiffening limbs to find his way to the lake's edge. With great effort he made it to land. His legs would no longer respond properly to his commands. He made slow progress as he crawled up the muddy bank. Resting a moment he drew his limp left hand to his wounded shoulder to find it slimy with blood. He applied pressure and felt spikes of pain surge through his body. He lay in the mud staring up into the sky. A shooting star caught his eye as it crossed the cloud filled heavens. Gary's vision faded out with his consciousness. He dreamed that he was safe at home in his bed.

What he thought was moments later, must have been longer because when he opened his eyes again the sky was starting to show hints of the impending dawn. Gary tried to move but his body would not listen. The canister slipped from his weakened hand and rolled down the bank into the water. Its heavy composition drove it deep beneath the waves. *I'll pick that up later, just a little more rest*, he thought.

Gary's breathing grew more and more difficult. There was a dry thirst in his throat. Every breath was a labor. The distance between inhale and exhale grew longer as his lungs succumbed to the inevitable. His body began to buzz as if it were stung by a thousand bees. His vision blurred. The view of morning sky above smeared into a grey mass no longer recognizable. The image his eyes sent to his brain suddenly faded as if someone had unplugged a television. He knew he was dying. He was too overcome by exhaustion to cry out. All he could hear was his struggle for air that seemed to be traveling away from him, echoing at a greater and greater distance; loosing volume with each tragic gasp. Gary thought that he was getting hungry. His mouth watered with starvation. Finally, Gary Jones stopped thinking; stopped breathing and his final comment on the world was a single tear that ran down his face from his open expressionless eyes.

Until, he got back up.

Two

Jack Mason stood six feet tall, lean muscled and tough. His dark hair fell over his brown eyes making him appear dangerous when he narrowed his gaze. This early morning in front of his tent at the Sierra Valley campground, Jack was trying to teach his best friend a thing or two about sword fighting. His friend of over eighteen years was a stocky thirty year old man named Tony Sanchez. The two men looked a little like brothers though no one could ever tell which one was older. Tony attributed their youthful appearance to their shared half Latin, half Caucasian lineage. Growing up together, the two often trained in many forms of martial arts as teens. Jack took to the sword at an early age. His studies of combat were buttressed by a simple natural talent. He took sword fighting seriously and wanted his street brother to do the same.

Facing Tony about ten paces apart, Jack held firm onto the handle of his bamboo practice sword with his right hand. He raised the rounded, somewhat harmless looking weapon towards Tony and spoke,

"Okay, this time I am going to leave myself open. See if you can capitalize on the mistake."

Tony sighed and held his *Kendo Sword* with both hands in a defensive position; straight in front of his body. He wanted a smoke.

He wanted a coffee. Hell, he wanted to be back in his tent sleeping but *Kendo,* the ancient Japanese art of sword fighting, was a reminder of a simpler time. He could wake up early for this once in a while. Tony took a deep cleansing breath, just as he was taught to do so many years ago and exhaled slowly, allowing his thoughts to wash away into a quiet calm.

Jack advanced with amazing speed. His left hand joining his right beneath the bamboo hilt bringing an increased force as it struck Tony's upraised sword. Jack pivoted on his left foot and spun, bringing his blade close to his body on the turn and extending it as he once again faced Tony. With instinct that he hoped looked like anticipation, Tony back peddled a step and caught Jack's blade mid-air. Jack feinted to the right, leaving his left leg overextended and exposed. Jack, who knew Tony to be a defensive swordsman, left an exploitable weakness in his stance. Tony missed what Jack thought to be an obvious opening. Tony backed off and resumed his defensive, sword first stance.

"You missed it," Jack chided.

"Huh?" Tony said while noticing he had stepped on a sharp rock. He shifted his weight to absorb the pain without conscious thought. Then, in a heartbeat, Tony had more to deal with than he could have imagined. He blocked Jack's strike from the right at a low angle, left from on high and again from the right. Pain rang out from behind his left hamstring as Jack's blade struck. Tony fell to one knee and put his sword up in instinctive defense. He looked to see Jack demonstrate his control of his weapon as he stopped his sword just inches from Tony's neck.

"Punk," Tony exhaled.

Walking away satisfied in his abilities but disappointed in his friend, Jack asked,

"Were you even paying attention?"

Taking a seat on the picnic bench that was anchored to their campground, Jack watched Tony struggle to his feet.

"Man, it's too early to pay attention," answered a defeated Tony.

He took a seat at the bench opposite Jack and drank the last of his tepid coffee from a stainless steel mug. Jack thought for a moment and decided to try some honest encouragement.

"You have to attack more, learn to think about offense and defense at the same time."

"It's kind of hard to find targets when you're swinging at me so fast," Tony complained.

"That's why we train, so you can speed up your reactions, to see weakness and openings," Jack said. He did not like criticizing his friend but he wanted to help improve Tony's skill. They both had their strengths. Tony was a dynamo with the nunchaks; two hardwood sticks joined by a chain often used by Bruce Lee in the movies. Jack never could master Nunchaku. Then again, the swirling sticks were too dangerous to practice on a live opponent. Jack felt that there was no substitute for the challenge of a real person. The unpredictability of humanity was the only true way to test and improve oneself.

"You could be better, you just have to practice," Jack offered.

"I am better, better than ninety eight percent of the general public," Tony answered as he put down his coffee. "How many people practice Kendo anymore?"

"Not enough," Jack said somewhat sad. "You should take it more seriously though." Jack stood and started towards his tent.

"Yeah, when it's for real I will," Tony mumbled. He finished his coffee and looked around for his smokes. Amongst the clutter of the picnic table; underneath Jack's copy of *Secrets of the Ninja* and Tony's *Improvised Munitions Handbook*, laid his pack of cigarettes. Tony noticed that the box felt a little light but was relieved to find two smokes left. He separated the pair and popped one into his mouth. Finding the lighter would be another matter. It was not underneath the men's camp fire reading materials. It was not near Tony's collection of obscure vitamin supplements nor underneath his motorcycle helmet that he had allowed to fade in the sun. Tony stood over the table with his cigarette hanging dumbly from his mouth as he searched.

"Here, it was on your bike," Jack's voice rang out accompanied by Tony's lighter as it sailed through the air. Tony caught the stainless steel Zippo and lit his cigarette. Tony saw Jack disappear into his tent and wondered what time it was. Looking out over their campground, past Jack's white late model truck and their two motorcycles on a trailer, he could see the sun, still low on the horizon. There was still some hot water on the camp stove and the thought occurred to Tony that he should have some more Coffee. He poured a hot cup and added only instant creamer. He opened a bottle filled with eleven different vitamins and amino acids. Each pill had an esoteric purpose that Tony resolved would help him fight off the effects of smoking, careless nutrition and the occasional hangover. Tony had previously filled the bottle at home from his supply of health products in anticipation of the weekend. He palmed the mixture and downed eleven pills with a large slug of hot coffee.

Cigarettes and vitamins, Tony never even considered the contradictions.

Tony smoked while looking at the books on the table. They were so different from the textbooks that he had studied at college. The Improvised Munitions Handbook was written in the eighties by the U.S. Army to teach field personnel how to create explosives from common household materials. Tony had bought the handbook when he was sixteen from a military surplus store during the Regan administration. Back when World War Three seemed like it was just over the horizon. He had read the book cover to cover many times and was reasonably confident that he had absorbed the principals of improvised explosives. The weapons and training all seemed like useless knowledge now. After finally graduating with a Bachelors in English just two months ago and now facing the prospect of finding a real job, Tony wondered if he had wasted his youth studying the wrong things.

"Do you think thirty is too old to play army?" Tony asked with a loud voice as he smoked his dwindling cigarette.

Jack exited his tent dressed in full camouflage combat gear. His tactical vest was neatly stuffed with equipment. A large combat knife hung on the left side of his chest with the scabbard fastened securely as not to snag on anything while sneaking through the brush. He cradled a very expensive black paintball rifle in his arms, always aware of where the weapon was pointing.

"Who's playing?" Jack asked.

Three

The bright sun continued on its westward course over the Sierra basin warming away the early morning mist. A short distance from the main body of the campground, away from the reveling and often loud local campers, stood a lone tent next to an old country squire station wagon. Marcia Dahlgren's mind danced in that small space between consciousness and slumber.

Since becoming a mother she had discovered an ability to multitask in her sleep. Her first acquaintance with this ability was when she had fallen asleep while her husband David had been watching football. Her dream had incorporated the sounds of the game coming from the television. That evening, during her nap, she had led the Steelers to victory over the Eagles twenty one to seven. Marcia found the experience quite pleasing. It was an exciting diversion from which she awoke rested. This strange skill had assisted her while her son grew up. She was able to nap while still keeping an ear on her child's activities. She could sing with purple dinosaurs or adventure with Hobbits while her mother's mind would let her know if her son was getting into trouble. As a mother, Marcia had learned to tell the difference between the sound of her son getting a cup of water and the sound of the top cabinet in the kitchen being carefully opened while sleeping. The top cabinet that held the chocolate chips she used in baking cookies. Her boy was clever and tried a number of times to gain access to the chocolaty treasure when he thought she was asleep. While taking a restful nap she could sleep through unimportant phone calls on the answering machine but bolt up with full awareness if the voice on the machine was family. Marcia was a mother and mothers could do that sort of thing.

She lay peaceful with her back to her husband in the warm tent. The familiar reassurance of her home brought pillow cuddled below her cheek. Her mind transitioned into the waking world ever so slowly, to the sounds of birds and a gentle lake shore. Her bladder was full. She tried to ignore her need to relieve herself yet the sound of the lake with its soft waves would not let her. She had remembered that David had been up and down during the night, clumsily exiting the tent in the dark to pee. *That will teach him to drink so much beer*, she thought smiling. This morning Marcia found herself a little envious that men could just pee wherever they wished. She would have to walk over to the main office to find a suitable restroom, David and her son could just use a tree. *It just isn't fair.*

Her husband was restless. She became aware that he was rocking back and forth. His body leaning towards hers, touching her back with a broken rhythm. Still half asleep, she opened her drowsy eyes and tried to discover through her senses what David was doing. She heard a wet sound followed by a slight groan. Her eyes widened at the thought; *is he masturbating*? She suppressed a slight giggle while her expression scrunched up as if she had just bitten into a lemon. *Oh that is funny*, she thought. He was feeling frisky last night but Marcia did not want to make love with her young son sleeping in the car so close by. She had agreed to let the boy sleep on his own but was sure he would get scared and return to their tent. Marcia did not want to be caught in the throws of passion. She had pretended to be too tired for her husband. *I guess I could join in*, she thought. Her mother's ear would warn her if her son got out of the car. She loved her husband and in the soft warm confines of their tent she would be happy to lend the old pervert a hand, as it were.

Marcia rose up silently, intent on surprising her husband by saying something romantically clever. As she turned she was startled by the form of a young man sitting halfway in their tent through the open flap. She became frozen with an otherworldly fear. Her heart began to race. The young man appeared to be covered with dried mud. He was holding a pear sized peace of torn red meat. Greenish black drool fell in ropy strands from his bottom lip. His features were distorted and slack. The thing took no notice of Marcia who had become as stiff as a wax figure. Her expression was one most appropriate for a house of horrors. Her breathing quickened, filling her lungs with the foul fetid smell of decay. The young man-thing took a large bite from its handful of gore. Teeth gnashed against the meat while bloody hands tore the remains from his lips. It looked at the ground outside of the tent and appeared disappointed. A disgusting belch escaped the thing's mouth. It sniffed at the meat it was holding and casually tossed aside the slimy mass of tissue.

To Marcia's unbelievable horror, the creature turned its glassy eyes back in the tent. Its gaze passed her frozen form without recognition and fell to David's leg. A split second passed and she wondered with the speed of thought why David had not waked to deal with this filthy stranger. Her fearful eyes welling with tears, hesitated to move. The thing at the foot of her tent picked up her husband's leg. It lifted limply into her view. The leg was missing a generous portion of the calf muscle.

This isn't happening. She was having a most vivid and horrible nightmare. For once her lucid dreaming had turned against her. Instead of adventuring through a fantasy dreamscape her subconscious had delivered her a vision of hell. The man she loved devoured by a mud encrusted demon dressed as a college student. *No, this can't be real.* She must have had a bad meal last night. Something she ate was spoiled in the icebox and now it was giving her a nightmare. It would soon be over and she would awake to make breakfast with her son like she had promised. Breakfast, with freshly bought ingredients to be sure.

The ugly devil wore a torn expression of exasperation as it dropped the tattered leg. Disinterested, it turned slowly towards the outside and sniffed at the air. The living dead creature that was once Gary Jones stood with some effort, its body wracked by rigor mortis. Marcia shuttered as the creature exhaled a loud dry sounding gasp. It shuffled with stiff legs, towards the campground; foot steps diminishing with the growing distance.

She trembled. Her forehead beaded with ice cold sweat. Shivering she lay propped up on one arm looking at the open flap of tent where the creature had been. Silently her mind screamed; *this must be a nightmare.* She had witnessed the absolute impossible and it simply could not be real. The stillness of her terror was shattered by a sudden inhalation of air from her husband. The sickening sound of gas being drawn in by phlegm choked tubes echoed in the tent. She craned her neck to see David's face. His normally tanned skin had lost its color. His features that she had loved so well for over a decade were drawn and sunken. She moved closer, putting her arm on his chest, her sleeping bag falling open with her movement. Her husband's eyes opened. They were dry and empty of emotion. He blinked apparently without focus. He exhaled a stinking vapor that made her retch but she did not withdraw. This was her husband; this was a dream. She could make him all better as soon as she got hold of her food poisoned imagination. His eyes moved. Some sort of dark awareness flooded his features like a monster suddenly realizing that it had been born; born again, to a living dead existence with only the most primitive of needs. He looked at Marcia with eyes devoid of pity. Her smell was fresh, somehow appealing. Without verbalization or cognitive thought, the creature that was once David Dahlgren wanted to consume the living thing before him. No longer recognized as his wife or a human being, she was food. That is all.

Mind numbing fear prevented Marcia from understanding what happened next. Her mind simply turned off. Her mind that was able to entertain her through naps and keep an eye on her child did her one last great favor. It robbed her of her consciousness to protect her from the horror of her husband's attack. Doctors would call her condition disassociative shock. She would feel nothing. She would have no idea that her husband of ten years had just bitten into her face, tearing the flesh from her cheek. She would not feel the slightest pressure of his teeth grinding with primitive aggression into her jawbone, removing the soft membrane of her skin. Her body silently submitted to the thrashings while her mind transported her back to the memory of her soft pillow, nestled beneath her cheek.

Four

Through the glass doors of the campground market Veronica Emmons watched two men outside seem to argue. One of the men was her employer, Andy; the other man was a mystery. What was even stranger was that Andy, a six foot four bear of a man, seemed intimidated by the much smaller man with frosted blond hair.

"Who is that guy?" Veronica asked her coworker Nikki Howe.

"Are you kidding?" the short blond asked as she drank a soda.

Veronica looked at her with eyebrows raised, reassuring that she did not know who the man was.

"That's Lance Richardson, his family owns the plant. You know; our sponsor for the match," Nikki said and finished her can of sugary caffeine. She placed the can in the trash and began stocking drinks into one of the refrigerated displays that lined the wall.

"How long have you lived in Whisper anyway?" Nikki asked without looking back at Veronica.

"About six months."

"Well, Lance is an asshole. He thinks he owns the place," Nikki said.

Veronica was familiar with the plant. She had not really made any friends since moving to Whisper California; populations seven thousand, however, she had heard about the plant in her classes at Whisper Junior College. It seemed that many of the locals worked at the ammunition plant, loading bullet casings and processing orders. The company had many government contracts and the ongoing war in the Middle East generated a lot of work. The Richardson Ammunition plant was the sponsor for Andy's latest venture, a paintball tournament. Veronica thought it funny in a sad way that a company that makes instruments of death was sponsoring a competition that turned mock warfare into weekend fun.

Andy and Nikki where the two people that Veronica knew best in her new town, but that was not saying much. She was not very close to anyone up here in the mountains of Northern California. Veronica had an almost self consuming goal of becoming a doctor and her focus left her little time for friends. Veronica felt best when working towards a goal. Her free time was spent reading medical journals or textbooks; anything to keep her mind off of her past. Taking a summer job at the campground store allowed her to stay busy and earn some extra money but she also got to know her coworkers. She knew that Andy had worked hard to put together the paintball tournament to promote his field. Veronica admired his determination. Andy had built the general store at the campground to serve campers a couple of years ago. This year, the expansion of his business had provided Veronica with a job. Since there were no classes offered in the summer that she needed, Veronica was thankful to have something to do.

Andy, his conversation over, pushed on the heavy glass door to the shop and entered. He removed the sign that read CLOSED and propped both the swinging doors open.

"Veronica is your drawer ready?" he asked his attractive young employee.

"Yes, were all set," acknowledged the tall dark haired woman as she shut the drawer to the cash register. A phone rang at the desk near Nikki who dashed to answer it. Veronica noticed that Andy seemed upset. She was very perceptive about others pain and felt compelled to inquire about his well being. Nikki's voice sounded, cutting Veronica off before she could speak.

"Andy, it's the Sheriff."

Andy sighed as he turned and slouched his way towards the phone. Veronica watched with concern as Andy looked so heavy with thought. The smell of perfume and hair products snapped her out of her musings as Nikki took her side.

Veronica, a very pretty young woman of twenty eight, studied her coworker and wondered why she was always so dolled up for work. Nikki was short; about five foot one, but appeared more diminutive next to the five foot ten Veronica. She had medium length blonde hair and sparkling green eyes. Veronica hardly had time to be jealous of anyone. Her logical mind knew that she was attractive yet; deep down she felt a little plain with her long brown hair and brown eyes. She thought about coloring her hair or styling it at a salon but it was just easier to tie it back with a rubber band as she always did. There were just too many other, more important things to do. She was working on getting into medical school and had too many demons from her past to let such superficial things to get into her way. She had to admit though, she was a little jealous of Nikki's large chest. Veronica was a B cup but being five ten made her appear smaller. Veronica never tucked in the paintball tee shirt that Andy had given the girls as a uniform. She liked to keep her shirt loose, where her coworker liked to keep her outfits as tight as possible. Nikki appeared very proud of her chest, something that Veronica was too shy to show off herself, but then again, she had different priorities. She resolved that twenty one year old girls like Nikki were into that.

Veronica wondered; *was I ever that young*? She did not think so; she had too many things to do when she was twenty one. Taking care of her dying father took up all of her time and her youth. As an Army trauma surgeon, her father had contracted a mysterious cancer during the first gulf war. He had lasted six and a half years with the disease as a testament to his strength, but also due to the love and care of his daughter. Her mother had died in childbirth so Veronica and her father only had each other in the world. But that was a lifetime ago. The insurance settlement had ensured her a small level of comfort and the ability to pursue her education. Veronica had moved to the country to evade the memory of her past. To escape the bustle of the city that seemed to close around her choking off her humanity. Here in the open air, amid the slow pace of a quiet mountain town, she could get her life together. There was a small college and fifty miles down the highway a larger four year school with a Premed program. Here at the base of the mountain, she could find herself. She might not find a man with all his own teeth, but she could find peace.

"What does the Sheriff want?" Veronica asked. Nikki shrugged her shoulders and made an unknowing expression.

Nikki returned to her work, leaving Veronica to watch Andy. Her rough life had left Veronica somewhat empathic. She had learned to trust her feelings. Right now, her feelings were telling her that Andy might need a kind ear. It was in her nature to be sympathetic. Helping others was the best way that Veronica could think of to honor her father.

Andy hung up the phone perturbed. He approached the girls on the customer side of the counter.

"Girls, over here for a second. I just talked to the Sheriff. Looks like a bunch of kids from the JC were on a field trip up north of here. They haven't reported back, so get the word out, if anyone sees any lost, hungry kids, call the Sheriff or the Ranger station. We got some worried parents back in town."

Out of the corner of her eye, Nikki noticed a group of paintball competitors enter the registration area in front of the store.

"Sure thing Boss," she said as she motioned towards the contestants. Andy turned his attention to the glass doors and waved a greeting to the men. Veronica had to ask,

"Is everything alright?"

"Yeah," he hesitated, "It's just hard to make all the decisions."

"What did that man want?"

"He didn't come right out and say it, but I think he was threatening not to sponsor us next year unless his team wins," Andy confessed.

"Oh," Veronica said studying his demeanor.

"I am not going along with anything dishonest. If I lose the sponsor, I'll make it work without them," Andy sighed.

"Your doing great, we are pulling in good money," she reassured and touched his wrist.

"Yeah, thanks," Andy said as he straightened himself to leave.

Nikki, who was eavesdropping on their conversation while pretending to stock the shelves, joined Veronica.

"Are you into Andy?" she whispered to Veronica.

"No, I am just worried about him. He seems upset today."

Veronica was taken aback by the suggestion. She had no attraction to Andy, rather a general human compassion. He was nowhere near her type. She was not even sure what her type was anymore. It had been a long time since she was close to anyone; not since before her father had taken ill. Veronica decided to hide her discomfort and turn the suggestion around with a dash of humor.

"Why, would I be getting in your way?" she teased the girl. Nikki rolled her eyes and answered sarcastically,

"Oh yeah, you know I want to climb that mountain." The two girls shared a laugh. Nikki continued,

"No, I don't think I am going to find my Prince Charming in this old town."

"Come on," Veronica countered, "there are some attractive guys here."

"Yeah, guys who like to play Army."

Veronica shuttered at the mention of the word Army.

"No, my father was a surgeon in the Army. I grew up on bases all over the world. Army guys are far worse than this," Veronica said.

"Well, I have lived here my whole life and I am sick to death of these idiots."

Veronica's attention fell towards Jack who was some distance away outside talking to a reporter from Warpaint Magazine.

"Who is that?" she asked nodding towards Jack.

"Some hot shots from the bay area, Berkeley or somewhere like that. They won the amateur championship for California last year," replied Nikki unimpressed.

The man was attractive, eye-catching and somehow interesting to Veronica. Maybe he was her type, but the mentioning of the bay area caused her to relive old memories, dispelling her attraction.

"I used to live in San Francisco," Veronica said in a quiet tone. Nikki looked at Veronica with interest.

"I was thinking of transferring to SF State."

"I'll never go back to that hellhole." Veronica's demeanor soured as she turned to restock a candy display.

Five

Within the confines of his parent's station wagon, nine year old Elliott awoke covered in sweat. His mother had allowed him to sleep in the back of the station wagon on his own but he had grown fearful in the night. Elliott had reassured his mother that he was old enough to sleep alone. When the night started to play on his fears, he resisted the temptation to return to his parent's tent. Rolling the windows up kept out the creepy uncertain sounds of nature. The comfort provided by his nighttime security precautions worked fine until the sun rose. Elliot awoke within a stifling oven of glass and steel. He wriggled free of his sleeping bag and rotated his body so that his head faced the rear of the wagon. In a heat induced delirium, Elliot wormed his sleep weakened arm towards the door handle. Opening the hatch flooded the vehicle with sweet, cool relief. His hungry lungs drew in the fresh morning air. Elliott kicked his pillow forward and snatched it up with his free hand. He brought the pillow to the very edge of the station wagon and laid his head down right above the bumper.

Elliot was a kid prone to strange positions. He liked to sit upside down on the couch and watch television. His mom would tell him not to, that the blood was rushing to his head. When she would nap while he watched the Power Rangers, he would rotate in his father's recliner and watch T.V. with his head hanging off the seat.

He did not see why it should be harmful. He enjoyed the bizarre perspective granted by watching a show while inverted. He enjoyed not getting caught as well.

Elliott gazed with sleet filled eyes to his right. With his head half out the open door he could see the lake. A boat motor started in the distance. People began to awake and go about their day in the campground. He could hear his parents starting to move around in their tent. *Good*, he thought. It was Sunday morning; that meant a big breakfast with eggs, bacon and waffles. His mother had promised to let him cook the bacon as long as he was careful. He had gotten to sleep in the car last night and now bacon. The responsibility excited the chipper nine year old. He turned his head to look at the ground. Being just a foot above the soft earth gave him a unique vista. He noticed pebbles of various sizes, a few twigs and the ridges of a half buried bottle cap. A pair of small bare feet entered his view. His mother's feet. He turned over and faced upward to greet his mother with a warm smile. The rising sun was directly behind her shuffling form causing her to appear only as a shadow. She was moving strangely. He rubbed at his eyes trying to focus.

"Mom, is it time for breakfast?"

Young Elliot Dahlgren was very lucky that he could not see her. If the angle was different or the sun obscured by clouds, he would have been driven over the edge of madness by her visage.

She had passed away from shock that stopped her heart yet her face was torn almost completely away. Her husband dined on her beautiful features the way a glutton might consume fried chicken, only the delicious skin. Her passing was quick though her appearance did not suggest so. The reanimated body of David Dahlgren had lost interest in her cooling flesh. His decaying mind drew him out of the tent to seek fresher fare. When she had risen she found herself alone. What was left of her still retained muscles connecting her mandible to her skull. Instinctively, she began to make chewing motions. Her nose was missing and along with it, her sense of smell. She left the tent with the purpose to feed.

Her lidless eyes now scanned her son. He squinted against the powerful sunlight, unable to see her condition. She drew closer, salivating dark green bile. If she could have smelled the boy, she would have found his scent irresistible, however some living characteristic he had still held her interest. All she knew was that she was hungry.

"Mom?" Elliot questioned with a slight tremble in his voice.

She fell to her knees before the rear of the vehicle with a disgusting starved moan. Elliott struggled against her claws and horrid teeth. His small cries muffled by her attack. He fought with the strength of a boy but not for very long. He died upside down, his mother feeding from the soft tissue that comprised his neck. Blood rushed to his head and then splashed on the ground.

Six

Mason strode with confidence into the paintball registration area just in front of the general store. Flanked on his right by Tony and followed by three other men in similar paramilitary gear and camouflage. These were, Gabe Duffy, Travis Jason and Billy Tate. The three men were new to the squad. The usual gang could not make it to the match so Mason improvised. This weekend, he had called up some new talent to mix things up on his team. They were called Team Blackjack, the name of any team lead by Jack Mason.

Gabe Duffy stood an inch taller than Jack but a little on the thin side. He had the slight athletic build of someone who might have played water polo or volleyball in school. Gabe wore a black baseball cap backwards to control his light brown hair. His hair was not too long but during stressful situations it would take on a curl. He did not know if it was in reaction to the humidity of his own sweat or some strange sort of scalp goose bumps. He just knew that he disliked it. Gabe had met Tony and Jack on the amateur paintball circuit, each time loosing to Team Blackjack. Gabe started up his team, the Healdsburg Hitmen with guys from his work. Travis and Billy were bartenders from La Visage, the restaurant where he was a Chef. It had taken some doing to get the time off but Gabe was the kind of chef talent that kept customers coming back. His employer balked at the idea of loosing three of his staff yet he did want to keep Gabe happy. Gabe had hoped to work with Mason on the same side to learn about his strategy from within. Maybe they could become permanent members of Blackjack and win some first place trophies. Gabe's team was good but Mason's was pro material.

Travis Jason stopped to tie his black sneakers. His friend and roommate, Billy Tate stopped as well. They were like brothers but they could not appear more different. Travis was five foot eight with a very fair complexion. His light blond hair appeared almost white. His best friend Billy teased Travis that he was melanin deficient. Billy was a half foot taller than his friend. He was a black man who had grown up in the same neighborhood as Travis since kindergarten. His hair was cropped very close and he had a fair amount of muscle, much more than Travis. Billy, who was more outgoing and jovial when meeting new people, would introduce Travis as his "albino midget brother". Though they looked very different; Travis and Billy were inseparable.

Andy stood next to a booth that contained an array of measuring equipment and a large CO_2 tank. A man in a referee uniform was filling Tony's air canister that powered his paint rifle. Tony accepted the tank and attached the propellant to the rear of his weapon then re-attached his butt stock. He handed the reassembled weapon back to the referee. Paint guns are just that, they are guns. They fire balls of cellulose covered paint, driven by terrific amounts of compressed air. At their lowest setting a paintball hit is sure to leave a deep bruise on the skin. An internal valve regulates the amount of pressure that is delivered with every pull of the trigger. Each field has limits on their player's gun pressure. Andy's field used a different system to ensure compliance. After verifying the settings were within limits, the referee placed a thin strip of foil tape across the barrel where it met the body of the weapon. If someone were to adjust their pressure on the field, the tape would tear. Should a referee see a gun with damaged verification tape, the player would be immediately disqualified. Finished, the referee returned the weapon to Tony. He switched on the safety and approached Andy.

"Blackjack, over here," Andy called out. He spoke into a hand radio as the boys approached.

"Five Minutes, are they on the field?… Good," he finished with the radio and spoke to the men.

"All right, championship match lasts ninety minutes. The team with the most members after that wins. Your opponents have already taken the field so you will be team blue today."

Andy distributed five small blue pieces of cloth. As the contestants strapped on their arm bands, Andy took notice of the combat knife strapped to Mason's gear harness. He pointed with is hand radio at the knife.

"What the hell is that?" he accused with the voice of an angry parent.

Mason was taken aback by the tone of Andy's words. What he had seen of Andy over the past two days he had liked. Andy seemed like a cool guy trying to start up a good field. If Mason had thought Andy was an ass he would have barked back and returned aggression in kind. But this was not the case. Jack quickly surmised that Andy's anger was misplaced and decided to keep the peace.

"My knife," he answered in a calm tone.

"You can't take those things out on the field," Andy said relaxing,

"We wouldn't want anyone to get hurt. The girl inside will hold it for you." Andy pointed his hand radio towards the door of the store. "Get your guns verified and let's do this."

While Tony and Mason quickly unfastened their combat knives from their modular harnesses Gabe gave them a look.

"You guys are Hard-Core," he said with mock praise.

Veronica finished labeling a box of supplies with a large red marker. She was on her knees behind the counter sliding the heavy box under the cash register. Retrieving yet another box she opened it to see what was inside. She labeled each box according to their contents. Nikki watched her curiously. She had worked with Veronica every weekend this summer. She thought Veronica was nice. She spoke differently than most people in Sierra Valley. Veronica did not have an accent, like she was from another part of the country, but she used words differently, more formal and clear. Nikki wondered how old she was. She did not think Veronica would mind being asked about her age yet she felt that it would be somehow rude to inquire. She looked young and healthy, yet seemed older. Nikki thought it strange that Veronica took it upon herself to label the inventory. Andy did not ask her to do it. If it was Veronica's store, then that might make sense. *Why volunteer for something when you could just kick back and get paid for watching the counter?* Nikki helped herself to a pack of gum from the candy display. She had been chewing Andy's gum all summer. She would have paid for it if someone had mentioned it, but no one ever did. *Perks of the job*, thought Nikki and placed a piece in her mouth.

"Hello," said Tony with an amiable cheer.

Caught off guard by his approach, the chewing gum in her mouth had yet to soften with her body heat. She placed a hand over her lips embarrassed.

"May I help you?" she offered, her voice distorted by the gum.

"Yeah, can you keep this for me until after the match," he handed her his large combat knife. She received the knife which sank in her grasp just a bit due to its weight. She brought up her right hand to open the clasp. Nikki pulled the twelve inch carbon steel blade halfway out of its scabbard, examining its dull non reflective surface.

"What do you cut with a knife like this?" she asked with eyebrows raised.

"History, tradition, the curvature of space time," he answered having a bit of fun at her expense.

"What?" Nikki questioned.

"Abstract concepts, I mean, look at the thing, it's very sharp."

"What?" she asked again with growing frustration.

Jack appeared next to Tony, casually laying his knife on the glass counter.

"Mine too please," Jack added.

Veronica, finished with her toils, rose from behind the counter. Her eyes met Jack's. The two shared a glance for a heartbeat.

"Hi," Jack said with a smile.

"Hello," she said while a flock of butterflies took flight in her midsection. Jack's eyes lingered for a moment then fell from her face to her hands. His face brightened as if he were struck by inspiration.

She felt quite nervous at the possibility of what part of her body was drawing his attention.

"Can I borrow that marker for a hour or so?" he asked, looking at her right hand with a growing hint of mischievousness. She had forgotten that she was holding the marker. Quickly, she replaced the cap.

"Sure," she said offering it to Jack. He took it gently, a slight pause before she let go.

"My name is Jack Mason," his deep voice said.

"Veronica," she said unaware that she had replied. In that moment something happened to Veronica that had not occurred for a very long time. Not since her life had been turned upside down by the earthquake, not since before her father had passed away, not since little Jordan Paul had kissed her after her eleventh birthday party. In that moment, Veronica blushed.

"Thank you Veronica, I'll be back soon." He turned on a heel, pocketed the felt tip and proceeded out the doors. Tony joined him and left the market. Veronica took note of the shape of Jack's butt under his camouflage outfit. Her expression was one of approval. She watched Jack walk towards his men outside. She wondered if he would look back at her. Jack turned his head, glanced at her, smiled and then returned his attention to his friends. When Jack looked back through the open doors, she felt another splash of adrenalin warm her body. She blushed again, turned to hide her embarrassment and pretended to sort through some paperwork.

What the hell was that? Thought Veronica; the adrenalin making her feel nervous. She suddenly felt a little stupid. She had lovers in her past; men that she knew, but did not really know her. Short term boyfriends in high school and the occasional blind date made up her past relationships. But no one ever truly close, certainly not since her father contracted cancer. She felt that she was a mess. The thought of sharing all of her neurosis with someone other than a trained professional bound by the protection of a patient-doctor privilege frightened Veronica. She worried that she may never let herself get close to a man. Loosing her father left her with an aversion to letting others into her life. She felt silly that such a small moment with a man left her flustered. *All he did was smile and be nice*, she told herself, *no big deal*. He was charm and testosterone and she wished she could get to know him. She wished she could allow a special someone to get to know her. The encounter brought up thoughts that she did not want to think about. Veronica noticed that her hands were clammy. Her thoughts were racing. The walls of the little market seemed to close in on her. She had not felt this kind of anxiety since before she left San Francisco. She needed a moment alone. Stealing a glance at Nikki, she could see that her issues had gone unnoticed. Veronica took a deep breath. Her throat was parched. She exited from behind the counter and grabbed a bottle of water from the cooler that advertised Cold Drinks.

"Going to the restroom," she said to Nikki over her shoulder.

"Don't use the outhouses, they're NASTY," Nikki shouted.

A local man clad in cut off jeans and an open flannel shirt placed a twelve pack of beer on the counter.

"Whose nasty?" said the man, his open shirt revealing grey chest hairs.

Nikki clamped her jaw down on a gum bubble with a loud snap.

"Have I.D.?" she questioned disinterested.

Seven

Timothy Erwin trudged through the forest underbrush cursing himself for wearing flip flop sandals in such terrain. He was relieved to get away from his parents for a while and finally smoke some pot. Timothy was fourteen years old; an age he did not enjoy. His parents did not think him old enough to stay home unsupervised. So he was forced to come out to the lake and spend the weekend listening to their childish bickering. He had discovered weed just six months ago and found that it made dealing with his parents much easier. Unfortunately his mother had kept him busy all weekend with stupid activities and trips on the boat. He had not had a chance to partake since Thursday night. The lack of pot in his bloodstream made Timothy think that he was experiencing withdrawals. He was cranky and uninterested in spending time with his parents. This morning he had finally convinced them to take the boat out without him. He had feigned sleep when they tried to rouse him and mumbled that he was feeling sick from the sun. Concerned, his mother wanted to head home early but his father said that she was babying Timothy. They argued of course, but eventually left him alone as he pretended to sleep. Once he heard the boat pull away he grabbed his pipe and headed out to find a place to smoke.

One has to be careful when trying to get high. Timothy knew that the other campers could smell the distinctive waft of the Ganja, so he would have to find a secret place. Smoking pot, or rather finding a place to smoke it was always an adventure. Back home he had devised complex rituals to hide his habit from his parents. He used incense in his room to hide the smoke that he blew out his window with the pretense of an interest in eastern philosophy. He even pretended to take up the hobby of jogging so that he could run around the corner and hide behind a liquor store to smoke. He left the house running, but always came home walking. His mother marveled at how his jogging had never failed to work up his appetite.

Timothy found a good place in the trees that he thought was far enough from the public. He leaned on a tree and fished his pipe and lighter out of his pocket. The bowl was already packed with some green bud from Oregon that had been floating around his high school. The senior he bought the pot from called it Medford Muffin Tops. Supposedly, the buds looked like puffy mushrooms filled with crystal red goodness. It was so good that a dime bag cost twenty five dollars each. Timothy tried some for the first time on Thursday night and was stoned for five hours. It was what the kids called creeper bud; it took effect slowly, creeping up on you. He lifted the pipe to his lips in anticipation, not noticing that he was salivating, lit it and took a long draw. The hot vapor expanded in his lungs. He held the hit as long as he could stand not wishing to waste any of the effect, and then let it out with a long relieved sigh.

"Fuck Yeah," he said as a dry cloud rippled from his mouth.

Three more similar hits passed over Timothy's lungs in the next half hour. He was developing a malignant case of cottonmouth. The pot began to work on his senses. Crimson spider webs of enflamed capillaries crept over his eyes. He knew his parents would get back soon and he could hide his dry eyes behind a pair of sunglasses. He would go out with them and hit some stoned waterskiing. Then he could have lunch. *Roast beef, potato salad and two fucking Cokes*, he thought. But not until later, eating might kill his high. The pot was good and should last a while but he did not want to loose his buzz prematurely.

Six months experience smoking pot had given Timothy an amateur standing as a drug user. He knew how to smoke but he had yet learned how to deal with strange events while stoned. The corpse of Gary Jones approaching through the trees startled him but he did not run or recognize a threat. The dirt encrusted form seemed unreal to Timothy's highly intoxicated senses. The creature paused and seemed to have a problem. It grunted as a terrible loud flatulence escaped the monster. A blob of unidentified black matter slipped out the bottom of the things shorts, plopping on the ground. Timothy laughed at what he perceived to be a hallucination. In the back of his mind he thought that he must have gotten hold of some laced pot. Maybe the senior who sold him the bud had wanted to trip Timothy out with some high powered shit. Perhaps it was laced with angel dust or dipped in opium. There was no way he could go back to his parents if he was seeing things. He would get busted for sure. *No*, he thought, *I'll stay here with my new friend Dirty McShittypants and hang out until I can get my head together*. Actually, the dirty man seemed quite funny to Timothy's stoned mind. The young man put away his pipe and began to laugh. The level of detail to what he thought was a hallucination was amazing. Timothy thought that he was going to enjoy the company of his new buddy.

The creature moved closer to the laughing boy. Timothy put his arms up like a person afraid of being tickled as he giggled uncontrollably. Monstrous jaws snapped shut, removing two of the boy's fingers. Laughter turned to screams as Timothy's trip spiraled into hellish torment. He tried to roll off the tree and back peddle but slipped in his flip flops. He hit the ground in agony, falling on a dried branch that punctured deep into his lower back. Timothy's life force flowed from his back, collecting on the slippery leaves beneath. The wretched beast fell to all fours and crawled slowly over the helpless boy. Timothy shuttered with shock as the putrid ghoul seemed to inspect his defenseless body with inhuman interest. The thing's gaze stopped at the boy's throat. Cold drool fell from its opening mouth, splattering on Timothy's cheek. Monstrous teeth grasped roughly at his neck, tearing ghastly chunks free with a hot spray of blood.

Eight

Team Blackjack entered the eastern side of the field. They assembled under the shade of the thick forest canopy. Tony drew a quick representation of the field from memory in the dirt. Mason liked the layout of the field. It was four acres of foliage roped off on three sides with a large slope that made up the south perimeter. Three referees were posted on the hill to help keep an eye on the event. They had headset radios on their belts to let the field referees know where the action is. There were assorted ditches and piles of earth in random places to provide players cover. There were many places to hide and strike from in this part of the country. He disliked the paintball fields that set up inflatable plastic bunkers for capture the flag style games, especially indoor arenas. Those contests forced players to attack each other directly, without any finesse or cunning. He would rather move around in battle, force his enemies to chase him or harass them with hit and run raids. Looking at the detailed map in the dirt he noticed that Gabe had something on his mind. Tony spoke.

"We haven't met these cats yet, but I heard that they asked every team we beat this weekend about how we work. Even bought some of the guys beer last night to hear the tale of Team Blackjack. We got to mix things up."

"How about you let us take point?" Gabe said looking at Mason, Billy and Travis nodding behind him.

"Eager for some kills?" asked Mason.

"We gotta mix it up," Gabe said smiling.

"Sure, walk the south edge. That will limit their angle of attack," said Mason as he indicated with the barrel of his weapon. "We'll stagger out on the north side. If we hear pops, we'll come running and catch them in a cross fire."

"Same here," said Billy pulling his face mask down over his eyes.

"What if we don't make contact?" Tony asked Mason.

"We will both hold at cover about 20 yards off the western perimeter of the field. If by 10:30 we don't engage them, we'll converge towards the center of the field, link up, fan out and catch them from behind," said Mason.

Gabe stood, affixed his mask and nodded in agreement.

"Move quietly," stressed Mason in a whisper.

"Come on guys, northbound V formation," said Gabe. The three newest members of Blackjack moved out.

Mason was happy. He liked those guys. He had wondered how they would be to work with, but they were a good squad. He had thought that Gabe, being a leader of his own team, might be difficult but there was no ego problem at all. They had agreed on strategy all weekend and made some good suggestions. They took their hits and did not complain; *not a sissy in the bunch*. Mason pulled his mask down and seated it tight on his face. He thumbed off the safety on his weapon and held his finger off the trigger guard, pointing forward. *It's game time.*

Gabe Duffy moved as quietly as he could through the low laying greens of the forest. To his rear followed Billy at a distance of ten yards. To their right spaced out another ten yards was Travis. They formed a triangle as they moved in unison through the brush. If one man came under fire, the other two could follow up with support. The blast of air released by a paint gun is very loud and would alert their back up to come rushing across the field. In these beginning moments of a match one had to stick their neck out to draw fire and find the opposition. A match where everyone hid and never engaged in fire would end without a prize. Not even second place cash would be awarded. Gabe wanted to make up the lost pay for himself and his men. First prize was fifteen hundred dollars, three hundred each. If he had worked the weekend he would have made more but Travis and Billy would have picked up less on their short shifts. Second place would still be good for them, but with gas and food for the trip, Gabe would be at a loss. He did not mind the money; he coveted a first place prize. Since starting up the Healdsburg Hitmen, Gabe and his men had always swept their part of the wine country. His team ranked each year for entry to the Northern California regional but every time lost to Team Blackjack. Gabe was tired of second place.

Walking point was nerve-wracking. Gabe knew that at any moment a high velocity paintball could smack him in the chest, the thigh, or worse, directly on his lightly protected hands. The idea of taking a hit in the face was fine with most players. The facemask provided good protection. He wore a groin cup during matches for the same reason but he had never had to test it. He was thankful that he had yet to get hit in such a sensitive area. Walking point to draw fire brought up these kinds of thoughts. He was sweeping his attention and gun barrel slowly from side to side looking for the enemy but all the careful concentration and quiet made the back of his mind busy. To the south he saw a referee on the slope of the hill lift a radio to his mouth. The ref was wearing his communicator microphone connected to his goggles, but still lifted a radio to his mouth. *Microphone malfunction*, Gabe thought and paid it no more mind. The enemy was out here somewhere, gunning for him; waiting to put a red ball of paint in his crotch and test the effectiveness of his cup. Gabe cringed at the thought. He wanted a first place trophy in the worst way. He wanted to make sure his men got some money for their efforts. But he also wanted to have children someday. He slowed his pace without realizing that he had done so and continued into the brush with greater care and focus.

    Tony followed on Mason's nine o clock, to his left and a little further back. A large pathway meandered through the trees, dividing the match field. Tony kept an eye on the path while staying in the thick foliage. He figured that their local opponents might lack the good sense to stay off the path. The enemy of the day was Hillbilly. These locals were probably used to hunting while drinking beer, rifles carelessly off safety, breaches loaded. The kind of guys who would eventually shoot one of their buddies by the time they had their second divorce, from their cousin of course. Tony knew better than to underestimate an opponent but he liked to make fun of people, even if it was only in his head.

    He noticed something through the brush to his left. Stopping instantly, he angled his weapon towards the movement. With his camouflage outfit and stealth he should go unnoticed. Tony knew that the human sense of sight relied mostly on movement. It was a leftover from our more primitive existence. When one looked directly at something the mind tried to make a connection from the shape of what it saw. Something man shaped was a man; something tree shaped was a tree, or so the mind told us. The broken patterns and random dark colors of his camouflage were designed to blend in with nature. It was not until you started to move that one could recognize the form as manlike. Movement, or the lack it movement, was a factor. Our peripheral vision is very sensitive to motion even in the very dark. If he stayed motionless, he should be invisible. He waited a breathless beat, eyes penetrating through the trees. A field judge walked down the path, oblivious to Tony's presence. Tony followed him with his rifle and smiled, removing his finger from the trigger.

The impact on Travis' back stung like an electric shock. It caught him dead center in the spine. The force of the blow sent small misdirected signals through his nervous system. Unable to control his muscles, he dropped his rifle and fell to the ground. As he fell three more blasts followed, one striking his shoulder adding to his pain. Billy whirled around to assist his best friend and caught a dose of flying paint in the forearm. It hurt, but he ignored it and swung around to return fire. Technically he was out but Billy did not want to give up until called out by a ref. He wanted to tap at least one of his adversaries. He fired blindly, dropping to one knee to minimize his height and profile as a target. He heard running foot falls to his left. Billy raised his rifle to the plastic mask that protected his face and took careful aim. A whistle blew.

"You're out," a referee hollered. Billy raised the rifle over his head, stood and allowed the referee to remove his armband. He cursed under his mask.

Gabe turned to run back to the action. A single burst sounded behind him and a split second later he was thrown off course by a Charlie horse in his right hamstring. Just below the butt cheek a flying red mass of defeat slammed into his leg. He fell to the ground face first, thankful for his facemask. He rolled to his back and looked up. He saw a hillside ref, blow a whistle while pointing in his direction. *Damn,* he thought, *where the hell did that come from?* Gabe sighed, switched his weapon to safety and threw it to the ground.

Moments after the first sounding of the battle, Mason and Tony sprinted towards the action. Tony was set to cover Mason as he ran across the path when Travis and Billy came through the brush on the other side. Travis struggled along with Billy's help. Gabe fell forward out of the brush limping. He removed his mask and cursed loudly.

"Fucking ambush," Gabe said passing a referee.

"It was like they knew where we were," he wondered out loud while looking at the ref accusingly.

Tony looked at Mason. The outburst was for their benefit. Gabe was trying to let them know that something unfair was at work. Mason lifted his mask and spat.

"Still got over an hour," he whispered to Tony.

"Change of plans?"

"Button hook east, stay in the bush. They are confident now; we'll have to reduce their numbers."

The two men made their way back deep into the trees.

Nine

Veronica splashed cold water on her face. Her nerves had settled with the change of scenery. She looked at herself in the tin plated mirror of the camp office bathroom. The mirror was made of unbreakable metal and did not reflect well. The image presented was slightly warped. Veronica stared for a moment feeling distorted from within. She let out a deep breath. It had been almost a year since she had felt that overwhelming anxiety. The strange sensation that she was not really in her body had not plagued her since after the death of her father. She grieved for a time after his passing. Soon after the funeral she had suddenly realized how alone she was. Spending almost seven years devoted to her dad had left her without purpose. She had things to busy herself. She had the goal of studying medicine but almost nothing else. Veronica floundered at San Francisco City College in remedial Math and English classes. She had to make up for lost time in basic courses to gain entrance to the classes that really interested her. With extreme patience, she labored to complete arbitrary scholastic tasks while silently suffering with her loss. She lasted a year in the city alone. Her last semester at SF City College, she had taken sixteen units. Veronica had shoveled education into her brain the way a fat kid eats a birthday cake; as fast as possible, lest someone else get more than their share. She had taken Intro to Algebra, Critical Thinking in History, Intro to Psychology, Biology with a lab and English. Her last final over, she bent down to tie her sneakers. The string broke low in her laces, leaving her no way to secure her shoe. She began to cry. Veronica had no idea what was happening to her. Her elaborate system of emotional defensive barriers seemed to collapse. The broken shoelace, a small and simple issue, was the last straw. The ride home on public transportation was a trek through emotional chaos. She pretended that everything was alright and to the untrained observer on the street that is how she appeared. Inside, she was screaming.

She had been uncomfortable in large cities since she was eleven years old. Since that October day when her father took her to a baseball game, her life had changed forever. They had gotten lost on the serpentine assemblage of concrete and asphalt that made up the Oakland, California highway system. Her father had just exited the interstate to a not so savory part of town in search of a gas station when the earthquake hit. The car shook so violently that she thought they had run over a patch of rutted dirt road. Her senses would have attributed the shaking to the car having a bad suspension if it were not for the loud rumbling. Her father pulled over right away and held her hand with reassurance until the quake ended.

The Loma Prieta earthquake measured 7.1 on the Richter scale. Moments later, several people started running past Veronica's car asking for help. The upper level of the Cypress freeway had collapsed onto the lower deck trapping hundreds of motorists. Feeling his duty as a doctor, Veronica's father identified his profession to one of the worried men. The man jumped into the back seat and directed them to the scene.

The earth had stopped shaking only minutes prior to their arrival at the structure yet one had to wonder how so much damage could occur in so little time. Veronica was stunned as she got out of the car by the number of cries and pleas from the double-decker concrete sandwich. Thick black smoke crawled out from the thin access in between the smashed road beds. A man had climbed up on the first deck, balancing himself on a cracked support column. He was yelling to another man on the ground to find a ladder and "something to pry the door open." He was a black man with a rough appearance. Someone that the young sheltered Veronica might have been afraid of in other circumstances, but not then. He was an everyday hero, casting aside his own safety to help a stranger. The man had tears of frustration in his eyes as he tried to talk to someone trapped in the structure. She would never forget the man's courage.

She was deathly afraid, not for herself or so much for those trapped, but for what her father might do. She did not want him to put himself at risk and possibly get hurt. She ran to his side and hugged him. The young Veronica begged him not to go. She did not want to lose her daddy. He knelt down to her level, like he always did when he wanted to tell his daughter something important.

"I am a doctor Honey."

"Daddy, don't go up there," she said, her lip starting to quiver.

"People need me."

Veronica shook off the cascade of memories, stopping up the passage to her past. She was desperately laboring to learn to become a doctor so that she could be there for others who needed her. She was there for her father in his final moments when he had needed her. As she spied her countenance in the distorted mirror, things became clear. She had spent a great portion of her life being needed. The encounter with the man in the store had revealed to her something that Veronica had a hard time admitting. She was too accustomed to putting others needs first and ignoring the fact that she had needs.

The bathroom was quiet and all of a sudden very lonely for Veronica. She wiped her face with a paper towel.

"I don't have to figure it all out today," she said aloud to herself in the mirror and left.

When Veronica rejoined her work in the store she noticed a middle aged man trying far too hard to engage Nikki in conversation. Nikki appeared to be reading a copy of the Journal of the American Medical Association that Veronica had brought from home. This caused Veronica's eyebrows to rise in an amused expression. Nikki never read anything more difficult than a Cosmopolitan magazine. People, US magazine or sometimes an Entertainment Weekly, however she had never seen her take the slightest interest in JAMA. Yet there she was, trying to pretend to be very interested in the magazine and not in what the man had to say.

The man opened a beer while trying to interest Nikki

"No open containers in the sales area," Veronica said sternly as she walked behind the counter. Dejected, the man looked at his beer. He meekly lifted his hands in a defensive posture, collected his belongings and walked out the door. Veronica approached Nikki with a knowing look.

"JAMA huh, Do you find the articles intriguing?" she asked.

Nikki put the magazine under the counter exasperated.

"Why do creepy old men always try to hit on me?" Nikki asked, and then spit her well chewed gum into the wastebasket.

Ten

Tony Block navigated the soft forest earth with careful steps. He moved with all the silence that his large frame would allow. Considering his size, he was almost catlike. Tony moved from concealed position, to concealed position. Just like in all the military manuals he and Jack had read as kids, he knew that you had to have a plan when you left cover. Tony had a plan, and it meant that for a moment, he had to be exposed. His protective eye goggles itched as they rubbed on his forehead but they had yet to fog up. Tony would need to see well to target the enemy during this contest. He had his eye on a ditch to his right and planned to jump into it once things got more exciting and they did.

Paintballs whizzed past Tony's right, humming in the air. The volley of plastic covered paint blocked his exit. Instead of jumping to his right and the cover of the embankment, Tony realized that the enemy had targeted the ditch as an ambush. Three of the enemy would push him towards the ditch, while the other two would zero him when he jumped in. Tony loved it when he saw through a ruse. He prized his intellect's ability to see what could be over looked by others. He flattened out and kept his head down. For the moment he would be difficult to hit. It should not be a long before Mason took his cue. In the sudden chaos of the battle, Tony adjusted his contingency to reflect the fluidity of the situation.

"Where are you man?" he said under his breath. Hugging the ground, he could not help but count the number of gun muzzles that were coughing cold CO_2 at his position. Three to the left and two staggered diagonally to his right. Neither had a good shot at him while he lay close to the earth. The enemy had closed their noose too soon. Three more paces and they would have had him. *Good,* thought Tony, *the gangs all here. Jack should be near the two on the right, not long now...*

With great stealth Jack Mason moved in behind the closest opponent. He crouched low, rifle slung close, secured to his body. The light sounds of his footfalls were covered by the loud reports of enemy paint blasts. Mason shot his left hand around his victim's facemask and with his right; he produced the large felt tip marker. Mason drew a dark red line across his enemy's throat. The man fell away in shock as Mason disarmed him, seized his weapon and put two blasts of red paint into his confused victim for good measure. The red team member writhed in pain as Mason dropped to the ground and used the suffering red team's fetal body as cover. The scuffle drew the attention of the other red team member nearby. Mason delivered two game ending taps of red paint to the man from his teammate's weapon. Jumping to his feet and racing towards Tony's position, Mason fired a spread through the trees across the path to cover his teammate. Tony, sensing that the time was right rolled into the ditch where he planned to reposition and try to pick off their last three opponents. Some where in the distance Mason heard a referee's whistle blow twice, indicating that two players were out of the game. Mason's smile was hidden by his facemask.

Tony moved in next to a large rock on the crest of the ditch, just underneath his friend's position. Mason stood behind a large oak tree firing the confiscated gun. It was his hope to disorient his opponents by firing their own color paint their way instilling the thought of friendly fire. Mason grew angry and wanted to embarrass his opponents anyway he could. He was glad he sliced that last guy's neck with indelible ink. The ink would take a long time to wear off and the shame would endure even longer. Mason smiled at the thought. He could see three enemy positions in the foliage across the path. He continued to fire while noticing that Tony had his back to the ditch, digging out something from his tactical vest. Volleys of paintballs continued to hit nearby as he voiced his curiosity.

"What are you doing?" asked Mason.

Tony produced a small mirror on a telescoping rod that looked very much like a walkie talkie antenna. He extended the mirror and held it above his head outside of the cover of the ditch.

"I got this at the flea market last week; I've been dying to try it out," Tony answered with glee.

Within the polished chrome of the mirror, Tony could safely see the tell-tale puffs of cold gas indicating where their enemy was. A loud snap caught his attention as a red paintball burst on the front of Mason's big oak tree. He looked at the spot where the paint hit. The impact had struck with such force that it left a deep impression where bits of bark had been blasted away. Tony looked at the tree from his position in disbelief. Something was not right. He had mentally accounted for the number of rounds fired by the other side as he watched in the mirror. The last blast was out of sync with the discharges from the tree line. From the damage to the tree, it looked like someone was firing at full charge strength.

"How many did you get?" Tony yelled.

"Two," Mason crouched down with his back to the cover of the tree. He could see a referee escort the two red team members off the field.

"Why?"

Perturbed, Tony once again raised his mirror into the air to observe the enemy.

"I think there are four bogies out there."

"What?" Mason mumbled in his facemask as he peeked around the tree. Three positions were still firing but their pace had slowed to that of harassment. It appeared that they were slowing up to conserve their ammunition for better targets. Tony squinted as he watched the enemy, taking careful count of their rate of fire. Without a sound his mirror tore free from his hand. It fell on the far side of the ditch covered in red paint. Tony's heart raced with surprise but felt a touch of exhilaration from having his suspicions confirmed. There was no way that shot came from either of the three remaining red team's guns.

Mason witnessed the event and turned his attention back to the referee.

"Hey Zebra," Mason called out. The white and black stripped official jogged directly towards Mason, who waved him off impatiently.

"Don't give away my position, over there." Mason pointed towards another tree to his right. The referee looked embarrassed at his mistake and complied with the suggestion. Tony sat casually in his ditch with his back to their foes. The referee stood at the top of the trench immune as a potential target. Shooting a ref was an instant disqualification for any player.

"What's up?" the ref asked.

"There is an extra player on the field," said Tony as he removed his safety mask to wipe his forehead with his arm, "and I think they are firing at full power."

The referee glanced across the path intently. He reached his hand to his belt and engaged his communicator.

"Critter, what's your twenty?" Tony re-donned his mask and watched the referee, not privy to the other side of the conversation.

"Sorry, Christopher, where are you?" The ref asked.

Jack backed up while still covered by the large oak and lobbed six paint balls over the path at an angle towards the enemy. He did not expect to hit his opponents but if they heard the balls fall behind them, they might get spooked. With the tree's large girth, they should not be able to see the discharge of CO_2 perhaps causing further confusion.

"I got two reds down, how many are you watching?" continued the referee. Finally he shook his head and said to Tony,

"No, everyone is accounted for." The referee backed up giving some more distance between him and the Blue team.

Christopher Baker stood in a small clearing dressed in his referee outfit looking rather nervous. He was speaking on his communicator.

"My name is Christopher," he said frustrated. "I am right behind three reds, everything looks fine," he said before switching his microphone off with a shaky hand. Beside him, lying in a prone position like a sniper was Lance Richardson. Lance was peering through the scope of a very expensive, highly modified paint rifle.

"Everything all right?" Lance questioned without taking his eye off the scope.

"Yeah, just a player count, but I don't like this," answered Christopher with a meek intonation.

"Take it easy Critter, It's almost over."

Christopher did not bother to correct Lance's use of his childhood nickname...

Mason had grown tired of waiting for the ref to catch the forth gunman. It was time to move. He figured that he and Tony should disappear into the woods for a while. The advantage would be theirs if they could use stealth and cunning to pick off their opponents yet again.

"Let's get lost, make 'em chase us then drop back," said Mason from his cover.

Tony was already tightening up the shoelaces on his boots. He had been thinking the same as his teammate. Risking the exposure, he stole a glance over the top of the embankment and ducked back down. The enemy did not appear to have moved.

"I am gonna need lots of cover."

"You got it, which side?" asked Jack.

Tony thought for a moment, He was pinned down for the most part with the entire length of his ditch vulnerable to the enemy positions. If he crouched and ran, he could launch himself up and out of the far left side and hoof it into the brush. He should be able to build up some speed in the ditch and limit his exposure.

"Fire right, I'll cover you once I get out," Tony said ready.

"Go!"

Mason's muzzle emerged from the right side of his oak tree. By the time Tony had started running, seven shots had ripped through the foliage from Mason's gun. Tony managed four semi-crouched steps forward then launched up out of the ditch. The impact came without a sound as his head rocked to his left. A paintball hit him mid air with tremendous force, throwing his body against the cold moist floor of the forest. Disoriented, he could feel a hot stinging behind his right ear, despite his protective gear.

"Out," yelled the referee, blowing his whistle. The ref ran to Tony and helped him sit up against a tree.

"There, did you see where that came from?" he mumbled angrily.

"No, it looked like it came from the other team," replied the referee with a sincere expression.

Shaking off the impact, Tony removed his headgear and felt his wound. A large bruise had risen up, beginning to throb. He grunted in pain and looked to his friend. Mason's eyes contained a bizarre combination of concern and anger. He spoke,

"You okay?"

Tony nodded with an expression of sarcasm, downplaying his pain.

"Looks pretty bad. Are you alright?" asked the referee looking at Tony's growing bruise.

"Yeah, I am just gonna sit here for a while if you don't mind."

The referee thought for a moment. The rules said that he had to remove fallen players off the field, or at least send them on their way. He had seen how hard Tony was hit and knew that a head injury could be trouble. He decided to compromise.

"Give me your gun."

Tony lifted his eyebrow in skepticism of giving up his weapon. He flicked the safety on while holding the weapon up for the ref. Taking the rifle, the referee spoke into his communicator.

"Crit.. er.., Christopher, I got an injured player out at the north lateral ditch. Don't let the reds mess with him when they come through." The ref cradled Tony's gun.

"Maybe you shouldn't be standing here. You're giving away his position," said Tony to the referee.

The ref nodded and walked further up the path. Once he was out of earshot Tony spoke to Mason through the trees.

"Do you still have the other guy's gun?" Tony asked in a low voice without looking in Mason's direction.

"Yep."

"Pass it to me," said Tony, putting his mask back on.

"You're out," Mason admonished, his honor at stake.

"I am not gonna shoot it, you are," Tony answered as he removed a compact Leatherman tool from his gear pouch.

Underneath the bush next to Tony slid out a paint rifle. It was a fine model, hardly worn just like the others that the red team was using. The foil verification tape was untouched. Tony kept the small rifle hidden beside his body. He sat the butt of the rifle under his leg and screwed the barrel off with his right hand, breaking the verification seal. He tried to look as inconspicuous as possible as he worked.

"We got some home cooking going on here," said Tony as he used his pocket knife to adjust the air seal to full power on the captured paint rifle.

"The refs are rooting for the locals," replied the invisible voice of Mason from the trees.

"Something is going on so I figure you deserve to put the hurt on 'em."

Tony reattached the barrel and slid the gun back into the brush. He looked into the forest where their opponents were, somewhere, and smiled. He rose to his feet and began to leave the field sure that Mason would find some measure of revenge.

Mason watched the tree line closely. He had never cheated at a match before. To do so would take away from why he competed. Not for glory or prize money but for the measurement of his skills against other competitors. Using the modified gun was not really cheating, it was payback. As Tony walked east, two gun barrels protruded from the cover of the path's edge. They followed Tony, tracking in step with his pace. Mason crept to his right and found an angle on one of the gunmen. *They are gonna shoot him and call it an accident*, he thought. Mason took aim with the captured weapon and fired.

The high velocity paintball hit his opponent in the facemask with such speed that it broke the plastic. Hollering in agony, the man went down. Two more positions opened back up with blasts towards Mason. He dodged through the brush to the west and swung around the cover of a large tree. He took aim once more and carefully chose his target. His aim went down the chest of a red team member where he hesitated for a split second. A chest hit would most likely take out one of these guy's ribs. He gritted his teeth at the thought. Mason was calculating but not inherently cruel, he moved his barrel down lower.

"Kneecap, Oh, this is gonna hurt," he said to himself and fired.

The impact hit a nerve in his enemy's knee joint. Like a strike to the funny bone but not funny at all, the man collapsed under the electrical sensations of searing pain provided by his knee. Mason laughed. He pivoted to fire on the last position and found no one there. He turned his ear to the empty forest and listened. Two men were in the distance crying in pain. The field ref was running to the scene. He could hear a boat motor in the far distance but no footfalls. If the last player was retreating he had made it far away. Mason's ears told him that he was either alone, or the man had stopped moving completely. The ref blew his whistle twice signaling two fallen players. Mason still listened.

A red paintball slammed into his shoulder from the south west. The blow spun Mason around a half turn but he did not fall. He steadied himself and leaned against a large oak. He had been listening for his enemy when he was hit but there was no report from a gun. He thought that there was very little chance that the last player could have changed angles on him so fast. *The fix was in; Home cooking indeed*, he thought.

"Mother Fu...," mumbled Mason. Disappointed and angry, he threw the commandeered paint gun deep into the woods.

"You got him, that's it," said Christopher.

"I know, I saw," answered Lance removing a foot long silencer from the barrel of his gun. He tucked the silencer and his rifle in a bag hidden under a bush. Rising to his feet, he donned only eye protection and fiddled with his blond hair so that it fell over the front of his goggles. He lifted a hand radio to his mouth and spoke.

"Clay, pull back and swap out with me."

Clay Morris, one of Lance's shift leaders at the plant, emerged from the foliage. He was dressed in identical clothing and gear. Aside from his prominent Adams apple, he was very similar in appearance to Lance. The only current difference was that Clay was the only of the two to wear a red armband. Clay ran to Lance's position and handed him the armband along with his gun.

"Get my bag and bring it to the camp," Lance ordered. He turned to Christopher.

"And you, you got yourself a job. Come see me tomorrow morning at the plant." Lance smiled a perfect toothed grin and jogged into the field with Christopher following behind.

Eleven

Clay Morris felt bad about fixing the paintball match. His remorse caused him to plod about through the woods. Along with the burden of his feelings he was weighed down by Lance's bag of expensive paintball equipment. Staying out of sight, he removed his camouflage gear. The only one who could see him at the moment was the south referee on the hill side. Lance had paid the ref off so there was no worry about him but Clay found changing behind a large tree to be just a damn bit embarrassing. He stowed his duds in the duffle bag and walked casually off the field. Dodging behind some trees and far out of sight of anyone who might see him, he decided to take the long way around. He negotiated the land until he was out of the camping area. Right now he felt like walking. Guilt was his companion as he cursed his inability to say no to Lance. He wished that he had never taken the job at the Ammo plant. He needed the money but it was a bad place to work. One had to be a yes man and an ass kisser to survive the Richardson Ammunition plant. A small amount of self loathing caressed Clay's soul with cold wet hands as he thought about all the things he saw there but never spoke out about. He wished that he had the strength to call the EPA and report the violations and moreover, the courage to tell Lance Richardson to go to hell.

Crossing the dirt road that continued high into the heart of mountain, he continued until his troubled eyes could see the lake shore. Doubling back towards camp, Clay noticed an older man in a brown tackle vest holding a fishing pole. The man wore a pair of headphones and bobbed his head to the music. Another man with a bad limp approached the unaware fisherman. The stranger looked like a bum in tattered sweats. His face and shirt were soiled with filth. Clay watched confused as the bedraggled man lurched with what he perceived to be much effort towards the fisherman. He heard a fierce growl erupt from the stranger as he fell upon the fisherman. Stunned, Clay watched the man grab the fisherman and bite his arm high on the bicep. Clay dropped the duffle bag without thinking and ran to help.

The stranger sprawled out on top of the poor struggling fisherman. Strained cries emanated from the elderly victim. His silver white hair became stained with dark red blood. His wounded arm hung across his face in a defensive cover. The stranger bit back down on the fisherman's arm, puncturing the tricep. The fisherman emitted a heartbreaking cry for mercy. Clay entered the fray fast. Grabbing the stranger's shoulders from behind, Clay tore him off the battered old man. Pinning the stranger to the ground with one hand he lifted his other hand high in the air to strike.

What Clay saw sent tremors of horror through his body. The stranger looked like an escapee from hell. He was not covered with filth, he was covered with blood. Caked and coagulated stains surrounded the stranger's mouth like a madman at an all you can eat rib house. His breath reminded Clay of the time a rat had died in his garage but no one knew where. A distinct smell of decay that grows over time getting worse and worse until it is strong enough to locate. The stranger's torso was covered with sticky blood slime, so much so that Clay's hand slipped off the stranger's neck. The blood encrusted specter lifted its arm around Clay as he fell, pulling him towards blood stained teeth. Clay fought with all of his strength to push off the ground, away from the maul of snapping jaws. A cold stink washed over his neck as the creature breathed out. Clay's arms shivered with fatigue, his hands dug into the soft earth as he tried to force himself away from the lunatic. The thing's teeth found Clay's Adams apple, crushing down awash in blood and flesh. The terror and pain coursed through Clay's body releasing a full jolt of adrenalin allowing him a momentary burst of near super human strength. Clay pushed off the ground leaving a part of himself in the stranger's mouth.

Clay instinctively put his dirt covered hand to his neck. He screamed in agony but heard nothing. He ran away, towards the campground. The pain was incredible but he was still mobile. He tried to apply pressure to stop the bleeding but the action made him choke. The dirt transferring from his hand smeared over his slimy wound creating a disgusting mush. He felt air blow across his hand as he tried to scream. He inhaled hard yet could get little air. He coughed but nothing came out of his mouth. Chunky slime shot onto the hand that he held to his throat. It was all coming out of his neck. He bent over as he ran and found that he could gain a little more air. The blood flowed over his hand and down into the dirt instead of going into his lungs. Looking back through tear clouded eyes; he saw that no one was following. He used what little strength he had to scale a small grade and gain more distance from his assailant. Clay struggled for breath. The gash in his neck started to swell from the injury. His torn air passage began to shrink from the trauma. The neck was bleeding but it was not squirting out in jets like in the movies. His run had slowed to a weak stumble. Each step was becoming more difficult. If he could catch his breath he could start again. *Just a little rest* he thought as he slammed to the ground. He slid an arm under his chest to prop his body up as he lay face down in the dirt. He had to let his neck bleed downwards to keep his air passages as clear as possible.

A horrible feeling descended on Clay. *This is one of those things that can't be undone.* Like when he was a kid and he broke his arm climbing a tree. He remembered how he thought then; if *he had only gone swimming instead of climbing the tree, he wouldn't have broken his arm.* Lying in the dirt now, he thought to himself that *he should have went and got the sheriff or something.* He should not have gotten involved. He struggled against his narrowing airway for breath. Pain and exhaustion overwhelmed his senses. A sad, high pitched sound whimpered from the hole in his trachea as Clay lost consciousness.

Twelve

Jack Mason entered the Paintball registration area as calmly as he could. He was attempting to suppress his anger at the results of the contest. Andy Walters noticed Mason enter and was about to offer a consoling word. He studied Mason's expression of controlled anger and decided that it might be best to keep his mouth shut. Mason passed Andy without a word. He did not believe that Andy had anything to do with the treachery on the field but this was his neck of the woods. *The man should run a better shop*, he thought. Mason spied Tony standing next to an old Volkswagen Mini Camper with its engine idling on the camp road. Mason stepped off the deck of the registration area and double checked the safety on his weapon. He was always careful with his dangerous gear around the public. Nearing his friend, he heard the last bit of conversation.

"Yeah, right across the dude's neck," Tony said smiling.

Tony was talking to Billy through the passenger's window. Gabe sat in the driver's seat with Travis sprawled out in the back. Billy was the first to acknowledge Jack.

"There he is," said Billy. Tony turned to Jack allowing him space to see in the van's open window.

"The guy from Warpaint magazine took a picture of the guy with the mark on his throat. You should have seen the look on the dude's face. He said he never heard of anything like that before," Tony said trying in his own way to help Jack look on the bright side of things. Jack faked a half hearted smile.

"We are heading down into town to see if we can't catch the Raiders game," said Gabe loudly, his voice struggling over the rapid coughs of the air cooled Volkswagen.

"Yeah, where at?" Jack asked.

"Don't know, they gotta have a bar or something down there," replied Gabe. Tony, bored with conversational pleasantries, caught a glimpse of blonde hair in his peripheral vision and turned to watch Nikki move about the registration area. He straightened his posture and pulled his shoulders back. *Notice me chick*, he thought.

"Cool," Jack answered leaning his arms in the window. "We are going do some riding later on today." Travis stirred in the back seat making an attempt to find a more comfortable position.

"Are you gonna live?" Jack asked. Travis mumbled an affirmative sound.

"Did you get your prize checks?" asked Billy looking at Jack.

"No, I'll do that later. I want to get away from that Warpaint reporter before he starts bugging me for the story."

"Well, sorry about the loss, but something was up on that field," Gabe offered.

"Yeah, I know. What can you do?" Jack asked with quiet resolve. He backed away a step as the van drove off.

Jack took note of his distracted friend. He turned to see where Tony was looking. The nice looking blonde was talking to Andy. Jack watched how she laughed and touched Andy in a clever but contrived flirtation. Jack could acknowledge that she had a nice figure however there was something about her that did not interest him.

"Dude, she's twelve," laughed Jack. Tony maintained his gaze on the little cutie. He liked the shape of her tight jeans and the mystery of what might be within.

"Nah, you have to be eighteen to sell beer to the public," Tony thought out loud, "She has got to be twenty."

"Yeah, well you're thirty my friend, ten years is a big difference. Eight years, that might work, but ten, not a chance," Jack said turning to start off towards their camp. Tony began to follow.

"Ten years is nothing."

Jack stopped and let Tony catch up. He looked at Tony's head just behind the ear. Tony stopped and put a hand up to protect his bruise.

"Are you sure you don't have a concussion?" Jack teased.

Thirteen

Ranger Jess Watkins' lower back was damn sore. He had been driving his Ram Charger up the rutted mountain pass for the past three hours. The dirt road was wide enough for Bureau of Land Management earth movers to access the mountain to maintain the surface. The last grading of the roads had taken place five years ago due to spending cuts. The constant jostling of the neglected dirt road drummed on his spine like a jackhammer. Today was supposed to be his day off. Recent budget cuts had left Watkins the only park ranger for this part of the range. His partner would normally be on today but he had been reassigned to Death Valley last month. His superiors knew that Watkins had only five months of service left before retirement so they gave his protests little consideration. When he did retire, they would send in some new recruits at a lower pay rate, but for now, the twenty four year veteran of the Department of the Interior was on his own.

The large patrol vehicle turned left off the mining road and pulled in front of a small shack. Watkins sighed as he looked at the well built building. It was a mining shack that once belonged to one of the families from town. He could not remember their name but they were the last to still hold an official mining claim on the land. The family did not own the land but they had the rights to any ore they found in the area. In the eighties an heir to the claim had come and dug out large parts of the surrounding hills in search of riches. It was the man's right to do so. The careless mining had left ugly scars in the scenery that broke the good Ranger's heart. The man never found gold in his search. Professor Galloway from the Whisper campus discovered the exposed areas of earth on a week long hike and had been using the area as a teaching resource for the past five years. The Professor was a good man and he sure knew his geology. Watkins was gladdened that some good had come from the unsightly greed inspired excavations in his mountain.

Watkins picked up his hand microphone and clicked the send button.

"City dispatch, this is Ranger Watkins, Come in?"

The radio was set to the Whisper police frequency. They were the only officials who could receive a signal this high in the mountain, through signal repeaters.

"Dispatch. Five by five, Jess. Have you found them?" The radio squawked. It was Annie, the sweet dispatcher from town.

"I am at the shack at the mouth to the valley, nothing to report yet. Radio gets bad from here out so I wanted to let you know."

"Okay Jess, how long should we expect?"

"Well, lets say an hour to get there and maybe 20 minutes to shoot the breeze with the Professor and see what's up, then an hour back to radio range. I'd say if you don't hear from me in a few hours, send back up," Watkins said while adjusting himself in his well worn seat.

"Ten Four, we appreciate your help on this one. We got a few worried parents who would like to know where their kids are."

"No problem, it's my job." He thought a moment and wiped at his brow. "If you do have to send someone, make sure they are in a vehicle with some clearance. A patrol car would never make it on these roads."

"Affirmative, Jess, good luck," said Annie over the low fidelity speaker.

Ranger Watkins engaged the motor and drove into the forest on a barely perceptible trail.

"Let's keep an eye out for some little brats," he said aloud, amusing himself. Professor Galloway and his charges were due back last night but by morning they had yet to show. Parents called the college who called the police who then called Watkins. They most likely had trouble with their vehicle and had to stay out an extra night without supplies. The Professor was no tenderfoot; he knew the land and would keep the students sheltered and safe. As a precaution Watkins brought with him ten gallons of gas, a five gallon bottle of spring water from the Ranger station and box of Meals Ready to Eat, provided by his employer. *The kids got a kick out of eating MREs*, he thought. He had boxes of the self contained meals issued to his office for disaster relief, compliments of the US government. They tasted like crap if you ate them too often, which Watkins did, but the kids sure did think they were neat.

The drive was long. Watkins knew where the Professor would set up camp. A large dynamited area within the valley that showed the stratifications of rock that the Professor was so fond of. "It is like looking back through the corridors of time", he would say. Watkins slowed the vehicle and adjusted his gun belt. He had left his .357 magnum in his desk under lock and key, opting instead to carry a lighter, more compact nine millimeter. His back had been giving him trouble lately and he knew the bumpy drive would be murder, so he decided to make every accommodation that he could. He felt there was no need to carry heavy iron to help out some co-eds. He would show up and give Galloway some gas, feed the kids and be back at the station to catch the Raiders lose yet another game in the final quarter. *No big deal.*

    Up ahead was the camp. He could see it was a mess; *College age Tom-foolery perhaps.* He had warned Galloway that the students had to clean up their messes when they came out here. Parking next to the large school bus that belonged to the college, he honked his horn three times to get their attention. He heaved his large body from the driver's seat and felt the miles still rumbling through his lumbar vertebrae. The sun was hot outside of his air conditioned vehicle. Removing his light jacket and leaving it on the seat he realized how glad he was that he chose not to wear his issue bullet resistant vest. *There was no need for that kind of protection on a milk run like this*, he thought. The burden of a vest would have only added to his spinal discomfort. Working through the stiffness of a long drive, he made his way to the rear of the vehicle. He heard the sound of many feet approaching. *Poor devils*, he thought as he opened the tailgate, *they must be hungry.* He reached in and slid the case of MREs closer so that he could distribute the food. As he opened the case, he caught a glimpse of a young woman dressed in a cheerleader outfit. *How cute*, he thought, *she must be proud of making the squad.*

    "I bet you kids are hungry," he said in his jolly voice.

    They were hungry indeed. When the screaming was over there was not enough of Ranger Watkins left to get back up.

Fourteen

Veronica reached down behind the sales counter and touched her toes. She remained bent over for a moment letting her back get a good stretch. Her emotional crisis earlier had left knots of tension in her muscles. It felt good to try and loosen up. She had a touch of a headache. While she stretched, she removed the rubber band that secured her hair. A brown curtain cascaded over her view. She exhaled while bouncing her body down low and almost made it to the floor with her palms flat. The sound of the door opening broke her moment of peace. Springing back upright her hair fell down upon her shoulders with attractive fullness. Nikki looked at her from the door.

"Hey, you should wear your hair like that," said Nikki, her green eyes seeming to smile. Veronica thought for a moment and looked at the rubber band in her hand.

"Does it look alright?" she asked unsure.

Nikki reached over the counter by the register and retrieved a large brush from her purse. She approached Veronica with a critical look in her eye.

"Yeah, it looks great," said Nikki with a touch of excitement. She saw Veronica as a quick little project; *good material to work with.*

Swinging around the counter, Nikki stood on two cases of over stocked sodas to get a better view.

"Come here," Nikki said smiling while brandishing her brush. She drew the large grooming instrument over Veronica's hair. Moving from underneath, fluffing a bit here and pushing other parts down. Veronica was not sure about this activity but she was curious. She never had a mother to show her the girlie stuff. She was Daddy's little tomboy and she did not regret it. But for some reason she was open to letting Nikki play with her hair.

"You know a trim and some highlights would be really cool," Nikki said finishing. She stepped off the sodas and glided with giddy feet back to her purse. Exchanging her brush for a small folding mirror she returned and presented the mirror to Veronica.

"Whadda ya think?" she asked with words so fast they seemed to string together.

Veronica could not help but smile. Her hair fell smoothly on the sides with a slight curl at the bottom accentuating the shape of her face. Nikki's mirror was perfect and clear; a sharp contrast from the dirty old mirror in the bathroom. What Veronica now saw was somehow encouraging. She was very modest and serious most of the time having little concern for her appearance, but her reflection at this moment made her smile.

"Nikki," she said.

"You like it?"

"Thank you very much," Veronica handed back the mirror. "I love it."

"I knew you would," said the little blond as she seemed to skip back to her purse excited. She put the mirror away and retrieved another piece of gum. "If you want I'll take you to a place in Baxter City sometime that has a good salon."

Veronica placed her hands on the counter. *Why not*, she thought. She had never been to a real salon with stand up hair dryers and all that fussy foo foo. She always had her hair cut on the military bases at the barbershop, until her father passed away. She looked at the excited Nikki for a brief moment and placed her rubber band in her pocket.

"I think that would be wonderful."

"Yeah," Nikki said grinning.

"Yes," Veronica nodded thoughtfully.

The moment of growing friendship was interrupted by Andy entering the sales area with a sour expression.

"Break time, who wants to go first?" he announced.

"Veronica, she wants to take her new look for a walk," replied Nikki.

"Okay, take thirty, when she gets back…" Andy froze as he noticed Veronica. *Oh*, he thought then quickly recovered and reverted back to his boss voice.

"..Nikki can take hers, uh, once you get back." Embarrassed, Andy nodded and quickly went back outside.

"Let me know how many guys hit on you," Nikki said as Veronica made her way out the door.

Nikki sat on her stool at the register and smiled. *I did good*, she thought self assured. Moments later Andy entered once again.

"What's up with Veronica?" he said, his usually deep voice pitching high.

"Just a little magic from yours truly," Nikki said with smiling pride.

"Yeah, not bad."

Andy was impressed. He took a deep breath and decided to get back to business. Consulting a chart on his clipboard he then looked at the large map of the campground. Double checking the clipboard, he pulled two envelopes from his papers.

"I need you to do me a favor. Take these checks to the guys at overflow fifteen," he said handing Nikki the envelopes. "Do you know where that is?"

"Way out there, but they have numbers on the campground, right?" she asked.

"No, not the overflows, Fifteen is the one with the pier over the lake."

Nikki turned and looked at the map on the wall. She had never walked out that far and was not sure where it was.

"Over the lake?" she dragged on appearing to think.

"Yeah, look I would do it, but I don't think those guys want to see me right now. Tell them I am sorry. I know that something went on today and that I intend to check it out."

Nikki moved around the counter like a child who has been sent to their room without supper. Andy retrieved the bag of knives from under the counter.

"Take these too, then take your break after, okay?" he said offering her the knives.

"Okay," she nodded unsure and pushed the door open.

Fifteen

Lance Richardson sat in his lawn chair dressed in a white tank top and khaki shorts. He was seated just to the right of his large tent on the shore near the camp office. Behind him were his favorite four wheel drive truck and his 1994 Porsche that he had received for graduation. The vehicles were parked bumper to bumper, forming a wall to separate his camp area from the others at the grounds. Before him bobbing gently in the water was his speedboat. Lance chewed on his thin gold necklace as he thought to himself; *I have a lot of cool stuff.* A beautiful redheaded woman exited the tent dressed in a blue two piece bathing suit. Lance watched Wanda lay out her towel. She got on her knees to smooth out its surface. Bent over on all fours he studied her chest. *Those are mine too*, he thought, having spent five grand on her breast augmentation surgery just last year. As Wanda stretched out for a tan, he studied her bottom. Wanda had a toned physique from all her daily toils in the gym but the bathing suit bottoms she wore did not meet with his approval.

"Why don't you wear a G string?" his question sounding more like an accusation.

"I don't like strangers staring at me," she said turning her cat's eye sunglasses towards Lance.

"Well, I don't like looking at big tan lines on your ass."

Wanda turned her head away and relaxed without a reply.

Lance was in a bad mood most of the time. He was one of those unfortunate souls who had everything and discovered that it was not enough. He had a good career as the quarterback for his high school team and played second string in college. He bought his position on the team. He had traded the original second string quarterback a Harley Davidson motorcycle in exchange for the man's cooperation that led to Lance's elevation to second string. He always had the best looking girlfriend around yet was never faithful. Lance owned many things and many people and still found time to be angry at the world.

Two men approached the secluded camp. Josh, a young man with a brand new black eye, was the first to enter. Zeke, an awkward man with a red line across his throat, followed. They took a seat facing Lance on the built in picnic table. The two men, as usual, waited for Lance to speak.

"Don't you two look like shit?" Lance asked laughing.

"He marked us boss," said Josh, the other man was silent with embarrassment.

"He marked you two, not me," replied Lance dismissively.

"He stole my gun," said Zeke meekly feeling at the ink line on his neck.

"Their buddies left, it's just the two of them," suggested Josh.

Lance glared curiously at his employees. He turned and looked to his truck. His shotgun sat in the window rack. He had no intention of using it but he was not above scaring someone.

"Just two huh?" asked Lance while looking Josh directly in the eye.

"Yep."

"Okay, let's do some business," Lance said as he stood. He looked at Wanda and decided against speaking. She did not deserve a goodbye. Wanda ignored the men as they got into the truck. Without moving her head she lifted up a small remote control. Pointing the remote at the Porsche, she pushed a button. The automobile's sound system erupted into a cacophony of loud music. Lance looked at her again as he drove off. He really did not like that bathing suit.

"I hope they kick your arrogant ass," she said aloud.

Wanda did not love Lance. Sometimes she wondered why she was with him. Life with him was fine as long as he left her alone. They did not share a relationship, they shared an arrangement. Wanda was his girlfriend and that could be fun at times. She was not stupid, she knew he was unfaithful. However, every time he messed up, she would get some sort of restitution. She had received a necklace, a laptop and a trip to Europe over their three year relationship. Every time he cheated, she reaped the benefits. Lying in the warm sun, Wanda was thankful that he had not yet proposed. Her life with Lance was fine for now, but she would not actually want to marry him.

Wanda felt her bottom grow cold. The sun was very warm yet something blocked the heat from her butt. Turning to look, she was surprised to see a male child standing over her. *Little pervert*, she thought, suddenly feeling very exposed. The child's shirt was torn at the neck and hung in shreds from one shoulder. A sliver of thick drool fell like syrup from his mouth. He sprang on her posterior. The boy sank his teeth just underneath her right butt cheek. He was small and fast but not very strong. Wanda rolled over, pulling away from the boy causing her wound to open further. His teeth punctured her skin but did not manage to tear away her tanned flesh. She launched a well practiced Tae Bo kick and struck the small boy, sending him down the shore.

"You little bastard!" she screamed, holding her stinging leg. The boy lurched back to his feet and rushed at her. Wanda flew into the Porsche and locked the door. The boy threw himself on the driver's side with an unholy guttural growl. His bloody torso left dark smears on the glass. Chunks of his little chest were missing and parts of his ribcage were visible. He pressed himself against the window face first and appeared to be trying to bite the glass.

In a panic, Wanda started the car. As she worked the clutch in to engage the motor her bleeding leg slid about on the leather seat. She looked at the boy one last time and let out the clutch. The little savage fell to the ground as her wheels spun on the dirt pulling away.

Wanda was in pain and extreme worry. She had worked hard on her body, *now some little freak takes a bite out of my ass*. She prayed that there would not be a scar. The warmth of her blood pooling in her seat felt like she had peed herself. She considered telling someone at the office that there was an insane little maniac on the loose but she was too afraid to get out of the car. She remembered the story of Martin Boone and how he almost died from tetanus when he stepped on a rusty nail at the plant. Infections could be deadly. No, she would go to the hospital first and make a police report. Her cell phone would not work until she hit town. She might as well call from the hospital. There were plenty of strong men at the campground. Wanda resolved that someone would grab the little bastard. Swinging the Porsche around at forty miles an hour, the wheels caught the pavement with a shriek and she rocketed out the narrow passage of the camp gate.

Sixteen

Veronica walked with a small portion of newly discovered pride. She was not ready to go strutting down the beach in search of men but her new hairstyle had given her a much needed boost. Lost in thought, she walked along the quiet main road of the campground. As she strolled she looked out over the vast recreation area. It was around noon and there were still plenty of campers down the long lake shore to her right. The sun shimmered in the water. People were having fun going about the business of doing nothing particularly important. She breathed in the fresh air. Her soul once again found the peace that was broken just a couple of hours ago by her feelings of loneliness. It was time for her to let go of her past pain and try to find something special for herself. For some reason she felt that she could now move on. Medical school was still a priority but there was no reason that she could not have a life and relationship along with her goals. This place was so much better for her than San Francisco. The shining sun, the sound of birds along with the clean air helped her forget the noise and constant claustrophobia of her former home. A small smile showed on her face as she walked.

Rounding a corner she realized that she had walked further than she had ever explored. The sounds of boom boxes and personal water craft had diminished with her distance from the camps. She turned and saw that the general store was quite far away now. She thought that she should head back but the quiet was soothing. The peaceful view encouraged her that despite her issues, she was going to be alright. Just like every horrible hurdle that she strove with in her life, she would find a way to be happy. Veronica knew that is would take a lot of work and perhaps a very special man, but she would try to be open to new possibilities. She would try to let someone in and build something, somehow.

The stillness of her thoughts was broken by a gasp emanating from her right. Cold fear descended upon her heart as she heard the tortured wheeze once again. She knew that sound from Oakland during the earthquake. It was the kind of sound one can never forget; the labored breathing of a person in mortal danger. She froze and listened. She heard a high pitched bubbling sound, a churning of gas through bodily fluids. She pulled her hair from over her ears and listened carefully, hoping to get a bearing on the sound. To her right, deep in the brush, she heard it again, a squeaky gurgle followed by a gasp. She walked into the forest with only her ears as a compass.

Veronica soon found the source of the sound. What she witnessed spurred her into action. She saw a man lying on the dirt in a pool of drying blood. As she rushed to the man she visually assessed the amount of blood he might have lost. The pool was small but there were drops leading to it. *He must have been attempting to get to someone for help.* She knew that she needed to stabilize the man before she could seek assistance. Veronica also had the presence of mind to wonder if she were in any danger. Always ready to aid someone, she threw her own safety aside.

"I am here to help you," she said firmly, "I have to turn you over to have a look."

With gentle care she rolled the man towards her, cradling his head. She was not shocked by what she saw. She had seen worse in her time. The man's neck was indeed very serious yet she was relieved that the major blood vessels were still intact. She removed her shirt, leaving only her sports bra without a thought to modesty and placed her hand on the man's carotid artery. Veronica felt a weak pulse.

"You are hurt bad; keep this on your neck." She placed her shirt on the wound stopping his breathing for a moment. The man choked and a small amount of dark sputum blew onto the white shirt. She realized that his trachea was compromised and felt tremendous guilt. Understanding the nature of the wound, she rolled the man back over to his stomach.

"I am sorry, I did not know."

She placed her shirt under the man's forehead to cushion him from the earth. Veronica could barely hold her emotions in check. She almost killed the man by not noticing the severity of the neck trauma. She was so worried about checking his blood loss that she forgot the order of first aid. *Airway, breathing and then circulation*, she thought. His breath sounds were what drew her to find the man, yet she forgot to check just where he was breathing from. He did not have much time however she could not possibly drag him to the office. Care must be brought out here.

"I have to go get someone to help. I will be right back, just concentrate on your breathing, slow and steady," she said feeling like an idiot. She rose to her feet and began running towards the nearest camp.

The whistling inhale and gurgling exhale of Clay Morris's struggle to hold onto life withered with each effort. His brain had already been starved of oxygen for far too long. His body stubbornly persisted to provide for his survival. Overcome by trauma, lack of respiration and infection, he perished without even knowing that Veronica had attended him.

Seventeen

Jack stood near his Kawasaki dirt bike in the camp. He examined his motorcycle helmet very carefully, looking inside for small stowaways. Jack gave the helmet a couple of hard raps with the palm of his hand and peered inside once more. He was terribly afraid of spiders. There was little in the world that frightened Jack Mason, but small insects, especially spiders, were the exception. He never could trust a creature who wore its skeleton on the outside. Jack was disgusted by any multi-armed beast that sucked blood from their prey. It had been some time since he last rode and he worried about insects turning his gear into a summer home. When he was a kid, his father told him a story about a man who left his boots outside while camping. A scorpion, attracted by the convenient shelter took up residence in the man's foot wear. When the man put his boots on the next morning, he was stung by the creature. The story frightened the hell out of Jack. Since then he would always examine his equipment while camping. He had already checked his and Tony's boots, vests, gloves and now finished with the helmets.

Tony sat at the picnic table brushing his teeth. He spat out a long arc of toothpaste into the fire pit and took a gulp of water from a bottle.

"Didn't you brush your teeth earlier?" Jack asked.

"I was thinking about going down and saying hi to that chick."

"Twelve," Jack said putting the helmet down.

"At least twenty," Tony countered.

"Don't bother, here she comes," Jack said nodding his head up towards the path. Tony stood and looked. He could see the short blonde approach with hesitation. Tony quickly gathered up the Ninja book, the text on explosives and his cigarettes and threw them over his shoulder into the bed of the truck. He opened the door to the cab and looked at himself in the mirror. *Not bad*, he thought, as if his closely cropped hair could get messy. He turned on the ignition and cranked up the stereo.

"Be careful, we have been using the battery all weekend," Jack cautioned. Tony blew off the warning and sat down trying to look casual.

Nikki saw the two men as she came down the path. There stood a long pier at the end of the campground with no water under it. The recent three year drought caused this part of the Sierra Valley reservoir to recede. There was plenty of water at the dam that supplied most of the areas power, she had read that in the papers, but this campground was experiencing a drop off in water levels. Nikki reminded herself that she could mention the drought if she wanted to impress the men with her knowledge. As she approached closer to the camp she saw the larger of the two sitting at the table reading a newspaper. The one that was in better shape fiddled with a green motorcycle. *They look safe enough*, she thought.

"Hi, I have your prize checks and these," Nikki said to get the men's attention.

Tony stood and smiled, he took the checks and knives. Jack continued checking his fuel line without a greeting.

"Oh thanks, that was nice of you," Tony said smiling.

"Yeah, I am supposed to tell you that Andy, my boss, he said that he knows something was up and that he would investigate," she said seeming to be relieved that she remembered it all.

Jack stopped his tune up. Both men looked at her with a touch of skepticism. Tony broke the silence.

"We think the refs had something to do with it. We have seen stuff like this before," he said sitting back down.

Nikki took a step forward.

"Andy didn't have anything to do with it, he is good people," she protested softly.

A disbelieving sound came from Jack as he returned to his work.

"Have a seat. I want to ask you a question," Tony said. She brushed off the bench with her hand, fearing that her clothes might get dirty and then sat down across the table from him.

"I was wondering, if you don't mind that is, how old you are?" he asked with as much casual charm that he could manage.

"Twenty one," she replied.

"Twenty one," he said aloud as to be sure that Jack heard.

"Twelve," Jack called out, surprising Nikki.

"What?" she asked in response to Jack's enigmatic statement.

"Twelve Pack, she is twenty one, offer her a beer," Jack said cryptically to Tony. Tony smirked at the inside joke and played the interaction off. He stood and retrieved two beers from the ice chest in the bed of the truck. He offered one to the sweet faced girl with the green eyes.

"You are twenty one so you get a free beer. That is if you would like one," Tony said holding out the can. She thought for a moment, *how old is this guy*? He looked twenty five maybe twenty seven; *why not*?

"Sure," she said. Tony opened the beer and handed it to her.

"I am Tony, that's Jack."

"Call me Mason," said the disembodied voice. Jack stood up from his work revealing only his head and nodded a neutral acknowledgement.

"His last name, it's a football thing," Tony explained shrugging.

"Nikki Howe, Nice to meet ya," she said and took a small drink.

Okay, Tony thought, *how do I look casual yet interesting*? He picked up his paint gun, checked the safety and proceeded to undo the foil tape around the barrel. *Not the coolest of activities*, he thought, *but it might do. I can't look too interested.*

"What happened on the field anyway?" she inquired while looking at Tony.

"We think the refs were helping out the other side," he said thoughtfully as he set his gun down on the table. "Plus someone out there was shooting at full power."

"Full power?" she repeated. Tony took a drink hoping that he looked cool.

"Yeah, this foil tape is to make sure that your gun is set at a certain pressure, these things can really hurt someone at full strength."

Nikki considered this for a moment. Growing up in a town of seven thousand people one got to know most everyone. Three or four of the referees that Andy had hired worked for Richardson Ammunition. Lance was a spoiled little brat; he certainly could have set this up without Andy knowing about it.

"I don't know much about those guns, but I can tell you that some of the referees work at the plant in town," she offered.

"What plant?" Tony asked confused. Jack walked over to the picnic bench carrying a pair of heavy motorcycle boots. He sat down while hiding his interest.

"The Richardson Ammunition Company. We call it the plant. After the Gold Rush, it's the only reason there is a town here."

"Okay, what does that have to do with anything?" Tony prodded trying to get a clear picture of where she was heading with her story.

"Lance Richardson is the guy who won the match, Well Lance and his team," revealed Nikki with a smile.

"He owns the plant?" asked Mason with a sinister air as he pulled on his left boot.

"No, his daddy does. His grandfather built the plant here in the forties supplying bullets for the war. He helped build the dam and set up the power station. He got people to live up here by offering free electricity in the town," said Nikki, feeling proud of her recall of local history.

"I could see Lance talking some of the referees into helping him out," she said to Tony, "A lot of the town works for his dad." Nikki made an expression of sympathy that Tony found very dear.

"Spoiled little rich kid," Mason said to himself as he finished putting on his boots. He stood and walked to the back of his truck, contemplating. She continued.

"Lance likes to push people around. Threaten their jobs; kind of an asshole," she flushed.

"A bully," Mason said to himself. He looked down into the bed of the truck at his Katana; a large Samurai sword that Jack treasured. He had bought it after his first win at a Kendo tournament when he was fifteen. The sword symbolized honor to Mason. The blade was fashioned from tempered steel giving it great strength and a fine edge. Hearing the tale of treachery was upsetting to Jack. He always played fair and held distaste for bullies. When he was twenty two he caught a man beating up a woman outside of a bar. He put the man in the hospital without a second thought. During the altercation he did not even grow angry, he just could not allow that sort of behavior. The police were not too happy with his actions but they did understand. He was released while the other man was charged with assault. Sometimes you had to take matters into your own hands. He was serious about his chivalry. As he looked at his sword, Jack thought about personal honor. His opponent on the field had no honor, and he was a bully. A combination that Mason held in contempt.

"I heard the guy from the magazine say that you cut one players neck with a magic marker," Nikki said directing her voice towards Jack. She found his quiet demeanor interesting and thought that she would try to engage him in more conversation.

"No one has ever done that before," she smiled.

He raised the sword out of the truck and into her view without an answer. He turned his back to sharpen his weapon on the tailgate. His intention was not to be rude; rather, his mind was elsewhere. Her smile faded.

Okay, maybe I should leave him alone, she thought. Jack was attractive but the other man was approachable and she found herself more interested in talking to Tony. Remembering that the men were from out of town and would be leaving soon she wondered why she cared.

Mason was the first to hear the rumble of a vehicle approaching. He lifted his head and focused his sharp eyes on the road. Tony heard it moments later and turned to see a Dodge four wheel drive speed into their camp. The truck roared in and skidded to a halt throwing a cloud of dirt into the air.

Lance jumped out first with his companions following from their side of the truck. Lance was grinning with a self satisfied array of pearly whites. Mason lifted the sword up and left the scabbard in the bed of his truck. He hoped that he would not have to actually use it. Mason was practiced enough to defend himself without having to cut someone but accidents could happen. He held the sword to his side so that the men could see it as a deterrent.

"Whatcha doing with that sword, you fucking ticket?" Lance asked with a laugh. His cronies joined in. In Lance's town, whenever he got caught doing something questionable, the police just gave him a citation. He got away with a lot and his friends knew it.

"You never know when you might have to take some punk's head off," Mason half threatened. He narrowed his gaze to Zeke and the line drawn across the man's neck. "He knows what I am talking about."

Lance reached inside the cab of his truck and produced a Remington 870 shotgun. Mason recognized the weapon immediately. *A classic*, he thought. He bet that Lance was bluffing even though he noticed that the safety was off.

"I hear that Hoss, that's why I carry this," Lance displayed the gun proudly. Tony stood and dropped his hand to his paint gun flicking off the safety surreptitiously. Nikki saw Tony's actions and decided that she should try to intervene.

"Why don't you boys keep weapons out of this?" she pleaded springing to her feet. Lance seemed to consider for a moment.

"Why not?" Lance said as he threw his rifle on the front seat of his truck. Mason made a mental note of the man's carelessness with a weapon. Tony lifted his other leg over the bench and gave himself some fighting room. Mason saw the two other men with Lance begin to make fists in preparation.

"Three against two," Mason accused as he walked with a relaxed stride, leaving his sword on the tailgate, "that's not very fair."

"It's better than second place," Lance joked, looking to his men for approval.

"I mean, not very fair for you guys," Mason said as a matter of fact. He approached Lance with his hands at his sides. To the untrained eye, he did not appear ready for a confrontation, but with Mason's speed and accuracy he was more than up to the challenge. He planned to use his open posture to lull Lance into complacency. He only hoped that Tony would know enough to go after the other one with the black eye first. His eye was a soft spot. Tony could take him out of the equation with one solid blow leaving just the two opponents. Mason hoped that Tony would remember their conversation from the morning and have a plan behind his attack.

A woman burst out of the trees to Mason's right. Lance flinched back a step reacting in surprise at the sudden approach of Veronica. Mason however did not move. His eyes stayed trained on Lance ready for a fight. Veronica, fatigued from her sprint for aid, bent over and steadied herself with her hands on her knees.

"I need some help," she said through heavy breaths, "There is a man down the way, he is wounded." She stood erect confused that no one was snapping into action to assist. Looking at the men she surmised that a fight was about to break.

"Look, this is serious, there is a man dying out there," she said with a stern voice. Mason, still looking at Lance with determination, spoke.

"We can finish this later," his voice was dry and deep.

Veronica suddenly remembered something her father used to do in a crisis. He would order people to do things. In chaotic events some people needed direction. Her father had helped coordinate the emergency personnel during the earthquake even though he had no rank or authority over civilians. They listened to him because he sounded like he knew what he was doing. Inspired by the memory she decided to delegate like her father had.

"You!" she ordered towards Lance, "I need you to go call an ambulance, now!"

Lance looked at her, then down to her sports bra, and back to her face again. He smirked and turned to his men.

"Come on guys, the little lady needs an ambulance," Lance mocked as he walked back to his truck.

Tony joined Veronica with a look of concern.

"Where is this guy?" he asked.

"Tell them we will be down the road about a mile from here," Veronica called out to the truck disappointed with herself for forgetting that very important detail.

Lance drove the Dodge out of the camp as Mason watched. Finally he broke his gaze and gave Veronica all of his attention.

"What can we do to help?" he asked.

Tony had an idea. He whirled and moved around Nikki to the table. He retrieved a small pack from his pile of military gear.

"I need you two to carry him up the hill where we can meet the ambulance," she said with less strain as her breathing leveled out. "Oh, do you have a first aid kit or bandages?" she added.

"Got it," Tony said holding up a medical kit proud of his forethought. He moved close to the other three, standing behind Nikki. Her perfume was sweet and he found himself wanting to be nice to her. He put his hand on her shoulder to get her attention.

"You gonna come with us?" he asked. She turned surprised and nodded; a touch of concern in her eyes.

"Lead on," Jack said to Veronica. She started off with a jog back into the trees. The men, with Nikki bringing up the rear, followed.

With all the excitement no one noticed that the music from Jack's truck had been gradually quieting. As they ran off into the woods to save a stranger, the volume lessened and eventually went silent as the vehicle's battery ran out of power.

Eighteen

The guys at the plant called him Rickets. His real name was Darren Richards. A smart ass trucker who liked to nickname people gave him the moniker and it had stuck. He had just returned to his camp with a twelve pack, drinking a beer while he walked. His camp was just off the edge of the main body of campers. He had hoped to pick up on a stray woman at the campground this weekend and wanted a little privacy if he got lucky. Now the campground seemed lonely. The girl at the counter where he bought his beer looked like a juicy piece of ass but she must have been twenty years old. *Yeah,* he thought, *she probably didn't know how to screw yet.* But it would be fun to teach her a thing or two. It had been a long time since he was with someone that young. He remembered paying the girl for her time and expertise on a visit to Portland Oregon. He smiled a lecherous grin at the memory. He had hoped to meet someone older this weekend; someone with experience who did not mind doing the things that a man like Rickets enjoyed. He never found his prey.

Lowering himself into his worn lawn chair he looked out over the shimmering lake. He took a large swallow of beer and removed his flannel shirt. The grey hairs of his chest had grown more noticeable in contrast to his tan. He noticed how round his belly had gotten over the past few years. His delusional machismo told him that he looked fine. He finished the last of his beer in a single gulp.

Rickets leaned his head back with his eyes closed, basking in the sun. *Tanned fat looks better than pale fat*, he lied to himself.

Searing pain clamped onto his left shoulder as the corpse of Marcia Dahlgren bit into his flesh. His reflexes reacted pushing her away with a pained grunt. She flew back, a small amount of skin and muscle fibers remaining in her mouth. He started bleeding while his vision clouded with tears. Warm blood gushed down his chest staining his body hair. He blinked to clear his eyes and had difficulty understanding what it was standing before him. The woman lunged with surprising speed at Rickets. He back handed her with great force throwing her to the ground.

The commotion caught the attention of three nearby campers. Two young men and a young woman saw what they thought was a domestic dispute. The two men witnessed Rickets hit the woman as if it were second nature. They both ran the short distance towards Rickets and tackled him. Rickets' large body hit the ground, knocking his wind out. The young woman ran to assist what she assumed to be a battered wife. She knelt down and tried to reassure the creature with a kind voice and was repaid with a savage bite to her neck. The woman screamed a muffled cry. The creature chewed quickly, slime frothing from her stuffed mouth and bit the woman again destroying the jugular vein. The two men, dumbfounded by the situation, quickly forgot about Rickets and rushed to assist their friend. One man ran around and grabbed the creature in a headlock. The other man held the injured woman by her shoulders. Her wound was slick with thin streams of blood. She began to have a seizure. The man set her down and held her arms to prevent her from harming herself unaware that she was rapidly bleeding to death.

"She attacked me," wheezed Rickets lifting his face to look at the men.

"That fucking bitch bit me," he cried as he held his shoulder. He got to his feet, stepped over the seizing woman and kicked the corpse of Marcia in her skinless face. The young man holding Marcia was rocked with the transference of force from the impact. He lost his hold on Marcia and was pushed on his back. The creature rolled to its stomach stunned for a moment until it focused on the young man's shin. Marcia's mouth snapped closed on the young man's leg like a steel trap. He grunted a loud protest as he lifted his other leg to kick the creature in the head. His bare foot slid off her slimy face deflecting some of the blow. There was not much meat to be found on the front of the man's shin. Her teeth banged useless against the bone. Sitting up she turned her savage attention to the young man caring for the dying woman. The undead corpse crawled fast towards the dumbstruck young man. The young woman slowed in her convulsions as her life slipped free from her body. Rickets jumped on the creatures back while the bitten young man grabbed her leg. The living dead creature growled while it struggled inch by inch towards the frozen young man. She fought with the ferocity of a starving animal desperate to reach food. Rickets bulk finally weighed Marcia down so that she could no longer advance. He put the full weight of his right hand on the back of her head as he propped himself up, grinding her wet skull into the sand.

"Chuck is Kim okay?" asked the young man helping to hold the creature, his leg bleeding slightly.

Chuck only stared at the still young woman without reply.

"Chuck!" the man called out again.

"I think she is dead," Rickets replied looking at the pool of blood that now tricked off the young woman's neck. He looked back to the young man with compassion, "I am sorry man."

"What the hell?" demanded the young man as he stood, leaving Rickets to hold the struggling creature. He had a good solid hold on her head and managed to get his knee on her back. She flailed about with her arms to no avail. As Rickets watched the young man approach Chuck, he felt a wave of revulsion wash over him. He felt nauseous and a little weak from the confrontation. Rickets vomited a half a beer's worth of stomach fluid on the back of Marcia's corpse. His hot bile flowed down the curve of her spine and pooled around his knee. He fought back the urge to continue by raising his head in the air to breath in a deep breath. The sunlight caused his eyes to cloud up as sparkles danced before his vision. He felt faint. Turning his fat neck to get a look at his shoulder he could see that it was still bleeding. His sense of smell was hampered from the vomit that still clung to his throat but he thought that his wound had a stink to it. He forced air out his nostrils in a disgusting spray of mucus and inhaled again. There was a distinct chemical reek to his wound. Nausea fell over Rickets once more and he struggled to hold back the sick. He felt like he was developing a fever.

"Chuck is she?" the young man questioned quietly.

Chuck said nothing, bending to hold the woman's limp body.

"Can you go get some fucking help!" yelled Rickets to the young man. He looked at Rickets with the struggling creature then around the campgrounds. Some nearby campers looked to see what was going on yet made no attempts to get involved.

"Help!" the young man cried desperately, the exertion of his efforts causing him to feel lightheaded.

Nineteen

Veronica was speechless. Standing where she had left the injured man she could not believe what she saw. There was only a drying pool of blood and her dirty shirt where the man once was.

"He was right here," Veronica protested.

Jack squatted and looked at the blood. He guessed the amount to be at just over a pint. Looking down the grade he could see a broken trail of thick blood leading up from the shore. *All together the man must have lost quite a bit*, he thought, *too much to get back to his feet.* About three feet from the blood, Jack could smell something strange. A sort of ammonia aroma was in the air, similar to the sweat of an amphetamine user.

"Tony, check this out," he said.

Tony dropped to one knee and looked at the blood.

"Oxidized on the surface, the yellow stuff is the plasma, it dries slower, fifteen minutes to a half hour, I would have to disturb it to get a better idea but the cops might not like that," Tony surmised shrugging.

"The smell," Jack said having already made the same mental determination though not in so many words. Tony leaned forward a bit and inhaled. What he smelled did strike him as odd. The smell was different than what he was used to for blood. The distinct metallic odor was not present.

"Piss?" Tony conjectured.

"Not unless he was bleeding from his crotch, Veronica said," Jack paused to look at the dark haired woman in the sports bra; "It is Veronica right?"

She was distracted while scanning around the area for the man, a look of confusion on her face. She turned to Jack,

"Yes, it is," she said. Jack continued,

"Veronica said the guy had a neck wound, that's here," he pointed to the blood, "If it was piss, there would be a puddle about here," he moved his hand down pointing where the man's crotch would have been.

"Then his blood smells funky," Tony shrugged, standing back up unconcerned by the odor. Nikki, a mixture of fear and frustration on her face, spoke.

"How do you know what blood smells like?" she questioned.

"I worked in a butcher shop once," Tony said looking around.

"And I used to hunt a little," Jack said looking up the grade to the camp road. Surveying the dirt for foot falls he thought he noticed something.

"Maybe someone else found him and took him to a hospital," Nikki hoped aloud. Jack moved his eyes to the incline leading to the road.

"No, he got up," he said standing. He did not know how someone with such an amount of blood loss could manage to get to their feet. Jack could now see tracks to the road that matched the ones leading to the puddle. He had missed the tracks near the blood because the others were moving around the scene obscuring the evidence. Veronica looked to the ground and tried to discern if she could see any footprints. She could not see any signs of the man walking however she did believe that Jack could.

"Is someone helping him?" she asked.

"No, he is stumbling around a bit but its just one set of tracks," Jack said and started off up the grade. Tony caught up to Jack watching the ground for evidence. Finally he noticed a smudged footprint. The man was indeed having trouble walking. His prints were smeared and close together indicating a short staggering stride. Veronica followed to Jack's left with Nikki behind.

Over the rise a man stood five yards away swaying like a drunkard. He looked about dumbly with his back turned to the party. Veronica moved to assist the man. Mason placed his left hand out in front of her, stopping her with a touch. He was sure to direct his palm towards her stomach avoiding the embarrassment of accidentally touching her in an inappropriate area.

"Wait," he cautioned, intuitive alarms sounding in Mason's mind.

The man turned to reveal a gaping neck wound caked with dirt and blood. His unsteady gait froze as cold dead eyes focused on the four samaritans. The man opened his mouth and appeared to release a roar. The only sound heard was a disgusting rasp of gurgling air from the man's neck. Nikki yelped a small scream. Tony back peddled behind Mason and placed himself in front of Veronica and Nikki. The man moved his tattered form, unsteady on his feet, his arms outstretched towards the party.

"Take it easy man, we are here to help you," Mason said with his left hand out; open in a stop gesture. His right hand at his side balled into a fist. The man became incensed, screaming without a voice, just the passage of air over dried decay. He leaned forward and picked up speed. Nikki put her hands on Tony's arm and held on for dear life. Mason tensed like a coiled viper ready to strike. Veronica could tell that Mason was going to act.

"He is sick, do not hurt him," she pleaded. Mason sighed feeling that this was no time for indecision. He wanted to help the man but not at the risk of himself or his friends.

The bloody man lunged. Mason grabbed the underside of both his arms in a modified Judo move. Using the man's momentum he threw off his advance. The move would usually require one to grab the shoulders but Mason did not want to touch the man's blood. Veronica was right, this guy was sick. He had a feeling that there might be some possibility of infection. The man hit the ground, air forcing from his lungs escaped through his trachea sounding like a deep sneeze. Tony pushed the girls back behind him with his arms wide and kept his eye on the man. The man turned upwards towards Mason, snarling disgusting sounds from his neck. Attempting to push off the ground, Mason prevented the man from rising with a boot to the inside of his elbow, collapsing his arm.

"What the hell is wrong with him?" Nikki questioned in fright.

Veronica studied the man. His neck was slimy and covered with filth. Dark foam drooled from his soundless mouth. His eyes were glazed and dry. There were blue patches on his forehead that looked like blood pooling from rigor mortis, *but that is impossible*. She thought that she must be mistaken.

"Some kind of disease?" offered Mason as he pushed the man down once again with his foot.

"I have no idea," Veronica said becoming very afraid, "we should restrain him."

"Fuck that issue, I am not touching him," Mason grunted as he kicked the persistent man hard down the grade. He rolled uncontrolled to a stop some yards away. Mason turned to the group.

"We don't know what kind of bug that guy is carrying, let's get out of here and get the Sheriff," he said shaking his head. Tony nodded in agreement. Nikki was already moving towards the camp road. Veronica, torn between her will to help and the truth of Jack's words, hesitated for a brief moment. Looking down the grade she saw the man struggle to all fours and begin crawling like a madman towards her.

Veronica joined the others as they ran towards the camp road.

Twenty

Barbara and Ted Erwin beached their boat on the sand in front of their campground. Barbara stepped over the side into the cool water wondering where her Timmy was. She had missed her little darling on the morning boat ride. He was not feeling well. She wanted to go home but Ted wanted to take the boat out again. *We are losing our Sunday*, she remembered him saying in that selfish whine that he called a voice. As she walked up the beach to their camp she noticed her boy wandering around. *Poor thing must have been lonesome without his mommy*, she thought. He came running towards her. She opened her arms to hug him. Something was wrong. The state of her child frightened Barbara. He was awash in blood and lacerations.

"Ted, look at Timmy," she cried to her husband as he exited the boat.

"Stop babying him Barb," he hollered back in frustration of his wife's constant fussing.

Concern sat on her face as tears threatened to flow for her baby. Timmy ran into her arms. She received him without her usual worry that his condition might stain her blouse. She hugged him close. Ted drew near, catching the faintest of glimpses at his son's apparent trauma. *Maybe there is something wrong*, the father thought.

"What happened to my baby?" asked Barbara consoling.

Teeth bore down on her neck with merciless force, breaking Timothy's retainer. Blood erupted from Barbara's wound splashing on Ted's prescription glasses obscuring his view. Timmy held his collapsing mother's body up while her legs buckled. He chewed the flesh that he had ripped free while holding her convulsing frame. The bite was very large in comparison to his mother's delicate neck.

"Timothy! Stop that," his father ordered removing his soiled glasses. The creature was far beyond the capacity to understand any form of language yet his father's voice did call its attention. The blood covered boy looked at his father with stoned dead eyes and chewed in defiance. The meat was warm and slippery in his salivating mouth. Swallowing the flesh and part of his retainer, the thing disregarded his father and took another, deeper bite. Barbara's body contorted and jerked in her son's arms as he dug his face into her neck. Ted shoved his hands between their bodies and tried to remove his son. Timothy growled and held on like a wild animal. Ted was a small man with very little strength. He got behind Timothy and found better leverage. The boy let go allowing his mother's body to slump tragically to the ground. The boy turned and menaced an angry roar. Timothy grabbed his terrified father who offered only a pathetic struggle. Falling to the ground, Ted raised his arms to shield himself from his son. Bite after bite, his child continued to take little bits of flesh from his small arms. Finally, with no more strength left, Ted dropped his useless tattered limbs as his son tore out his skinny throat.

Rickets was tired. Fatigue chewed at his muscles as he strived to maintain control of the crazed woman underneath his knees. The young man with the small bite wound had left to go get help, leaving Rickets with a catatonic shirtless young man named Chuck and the corpse of a young lady. Rickets thought that they said her name was Kim. He shook his head. *What does it matter? This crazy bitch killed the young woman, there's no need to remember her name.* He was feeling very ill now. He knew he had a fever and his shoulder was starting to smell really bad. The woman underneath him sporadically attempted to escape in small fits of energy. His vomit began to congeal and cool around his leg. He thought it strange that the woman did not put off any body heat. She seemed cold, perhaps it was his fever making him feel that way, he hoped. Rickets had to get off of the woman and lie down or risk throwing up again.

"Hey man. Hey! Can you get me some rope or something?" he called to the crying young man holding his dead friend. The man ignored him.

"Chuck!" He exclaimed, "Please man, help me the fuck out over here."

Hearing his name shook Chuck loose from his catatonia for a moment. He turned to Rickets slowly with tear stained eyes that lacked recognition. Kim jerked in his tender embrace causing Chuck to turn his attention back to the woman. Her face was pale but perfect. He had always had a thing for her. His unspoken feelings for Kim plunged him into an emotional coma when he thought she was dead. Chuck's heart soared at the thought that she was going to be okay. He would wait until she was better and then he would tell her how he felt, how he had always felt, about her.

"Kim," he said with smiling relief. She opened her eyes and looked from side to side. Her beautiful blue eyes were now somehow hollow and empty. She looked confused, as if she were awakening for the first time. She focused on Chuck. He brushed her soft brown hair off her face with care.

"Are you..." Chuck whispered.

Before he could finish she struck out. Her fine teeth caught Chuck on the cheekbone. She dragged the top of her teeth down across his jaw like a wire cheese cutter, flesh peeling back and collecting in her mouth.

"Kim?" he protested in shock, his voice raw and horse. She threw her arms around Chuck as he tried to back away. Pulling him close, her head over his shoulder, she bit aggressively into the meat of his trapezium.

Witnessing the attack, Rickets had enough. He jumped to his feet off of the woman and felt a surge of blood rush to his head. Standing so rapidly had almost caused him to pass out. He made his way on shaking legs towards his vehicle. He retched again and disgorged while stumbling. Vomit splashed against his struggling legs. Rickets threw open the door of his van and collapsed in the rear loosing consciousness. He lay helpless with his legs exposed outside of the vehicle unaware of the sand covered, skinless face that soon found his limbs. The disgusting creature that was once Marcia Dahlgren tore into the marbled tissue of his calf. She fed greedily upon Rickets unfazed by Chuck's cries. After four generous bites, his body cooled to the point where she no longer found his flesh palatable. She rose. Her exposed eyes in their constant stare looked about the campground in search of more food.

Twenty One

The Dodge pulled into the empty campground. Lance exited his truck wondering where Wanda had gone.

"Zeke, go call the ambulance," he ordered as the men got out of the passenger's side. Zeke did as he was told and left towards the general store. Lance looked around the camp and saw the burnout left in the soil by his Porsche. Shaking his head at the deep groves in the dirt he decided that it might be time to take the car away from his girlfriend for a while. Lance liked to enforce his way by restricting Wanda's access to his possessions. *Teaching her a lesson* was how he put it. When she would exhibit too much free will for his liking, he would put the car in the shop for some unnecessary work. She did not have a car of her own and Lance was sure to never give her enough spending money so that she could squirrel away a savings. She would have to stay around his house and work out with Tae Bo videos or swim in the heated pool. She would get the message and would as always submit to his authority. *What else could she do*? She was not the type of person to give up her lavish lifestyle and get a job. Lance smirked as he walked past the tracks in the dirt.

Josh noticed some blood on Wanda's towel. The dark red smear stood out on the fine white terrycloth. He pointed.

"Is that blood?"

Lance saw the stain and laughed.

"She probably started leaking, that's why she tore out of here." Sitting in his lawn chair he resolved that Wanda might not have brought any feminine products with her.

"I swear that girl has two periods a month," Lance laughed.

Josh timidly kicked a corner of the towel over so that the cloth covered the blood. From behind the tent a small boy corpse emerged. Josh turned into the boy's path and collided with him. The little demon grabbed Josh's right arm, biting down hard. He screamed.

"What the fuck?" Josh yelled pushing the boy away.

Lance sprung to his feet. He saw the blood covered boy with the tattered chest launch again at Josh. The man ran around the truck and the boy followed growling. Around they came towards Lance who lifted his hand high in the air and slapped the boy hard across the face. The child fell on the ground with a solid thud. Josh continued running until he was back on the other side of the truck. Lance looked in disappointment at Josh.

"He bit me boss," Josh said holding his arm.

"You pussy, running from a little kid," Lance said shaking his head as he leisurely strode towards Josh. Once closer to his employee he could see that he had indeed been bitten. Lance looked at the man's arm and could see teeth marks under flowing blood.

A man clad only in yellow bikini bottoms that he really should not have been wearing, walked down the beach in front of Lance's camp. The boy righted himself on the other side of the truck, took notice of the man and charged. Lance watched amused as the man in the yellow bikini shorts began to run away from the snarling boy.

"What the hell is that all about?" wondered Lance while disregarding Josh. He walked behind his tent to get a better look.

The man in yellow was still ahead of the boy. Lance walked out further through the campground to follow what was happening. Another man presumably heading out for a swim crossed the running man's path. They crashed into each other and tumbled to the ground. The boy jumped on the men. It looked to Lance that the kid was trying to bite the men. The scene reminded him of an orgy porno video that Wanda had bought to spice things up in the bedroom. He shook his head at the scene unconcerned. *A kid with rabies*, he thought, *sucks to be him*.

A tormented scream from his left snapped Lance out of his amusement. He turned to see a man dressed in fishing gear on his knees attacking a tanning woman. Another girl, who must have been lying next to the poor woman, was throwing her weak fists at the fisherman. The victim rolled over and lifted her hands in defense, slapping at the beast. The young girl rose and ran to Lance. He started to move closer out of some unbelievable curiosity. The girl held onto Lance and moved behind him.

"Help my Mom," she begged. The struggling woman, bloody and scraped in several places, pushed the man off of her and crawled underneath a Jeep for protection. The creature swiped at her calf with a bloody claw.

"Do something!" the girl screamed. The fisherman, attracted by the girl's pleas, craned its stiff neck towards Lance. It rose to its feet. Lance could not believe what he was seeing. The man was still chewing bits of the woman. The girl cried hysterically, holding on to Lance's arm. The creature began to advance when Lance whirled, grabbed the girl and threw her in front of the creature. Lance turned and ran to the tune of the girl's cries.

Lance passed Josh who was still holding his arm up as if to display it for review. He jumped into his truck and started the engine. Josh opened the passenger's side and almost fell out of the truck when Lance pulled away. As Lance carelessly drove through the campground he was cut off by a Mercury sedan that slammed into the camp gate at high speed. Behind the Mercury, a Honda Civic swerved and spun out, smashing into the Mercury's rear end. A chain reaction of cars followed creating a pile up that effectively blocked exit through the gate. Lance threw the truck into reverse.

"There's Zeke," Josh said pointing his bleeding arm.

"Fuck him," Lance said pulling a tight U turn. He saw Zeke waving in his rear view and decided to stop. He might need some manpower. Josh opened the door for Zeke who dove in the cab.

"What the hell is going on?" Zeke mumbled; his mouth full of chewing tobacco.

Lance did not answer. He pulled his truck down the grade towards the water and parked with the engine running. Through the windshield he could see most of the campground. He retrieved his shotgun from the rack.

"What are we doing?" asked Josh, feeling nauseous.

"I wanna see something," Lance said with his attention on the camp, "Open the glove box and hand me the shotgun shells."

Andy Walters heard the sound of the crash from inside his store. As the lights went out, he grabbed a fire extinguisher from the wall and shot out the door to see if he could help. A black sedan had smashed into the booth that divided the lanes in and out of the camp. A Honda had wedged sideways against the gate on the incoming lane, broadsided by a gaudy black and gold El Camino. People yelled and ran about in disordered pandemonium. Other cars, lined up behind the wreck were abandoned by their passengers. Andy looked about unsure of what was occurring. A frightened girl in only a bathing suit ran towards Andy screaming. She was being pursued by an older man dressed in fishing gear. The man stretched his arms out and seemed to be growling. Andy side stepped and allowed the girl to enter his store. Without hesitation he lifted the butt end of the fire extinguisher and hit the fisherman in the forehead with a hollow thump. The fisherman's body continued with its momentum but his head remained in place. He hit the surface of the deck hard.

Andy, seeing no one else approaching, turned and entered his store.

"Are you okay?" he said to the crying girl. He knelt down and set aside the fire extinguisher. The girl was missing the top of her right ear. It was bloody and obviously painful.

"Shit, what happened?" he questioned quietly.

"That man killed my mom, then… then…" tears took the place of speech, Andy understood.

"Calm down, you're safe now," he said not knowing if it were true.

The door opened with a jarring rattle, a man entered.

"Call the police," he said halfway in the door. Arms reached in and grabbed the man from behind pulling him outside. Andy thought he saw the fisherman back on his feet through the glass door. He reached over the counter and picked up his phone. It was dead. The lines ran from his shop to the entrance booth then to the pole outside of camp. The crashed cars had taken out the power and the phones.

The girl remained huddled on the floor in a corner crying. He peered out the door and saw more chaos. The fisherman and his victim were nowhere to be seen. Andy saw the reporter from Warpaint magazine lying on the ground near the registration area twitching in a puddle of his own blood.

"Holy Shit," he said and locked the doors.

Twenty Two

Mason led the group down the camp road at a medium jog. The girl, Nikki, seemed to be having a little trouble keeping up. He thought it best to keep the group together. He had no idea how fast the injured man could move or if he was giving chase but he was not about to leave one of the girls behind to get hurt. He knew Tony would keep pace with the young lady and stick by her. He could see where that situation was headed. Tony was the world's biggest sucker for pretty blonds so that meant that Mason would stay close as well.

The campsites were now in view. They had just passed the dirt path to their camp. Mason surmised that the office was still half a mile off. To the left, about fifty yards ahead, a woman ran into the road crying and pleading for help. *That is weird*, Tony thought. Suddenly a teenage male ran after the woman. The teen leapt on the woman and brought her down. She wore only shorts and a tank top. Her exposed knees and palms hit the pavement with a horrible scrape that hurt to witness. The teen ravaged her from on top of her back and seemed to be biting her shoulder.

Mason broke into a full run with Tony following. The screams for mercy from the woman were heartbreaking. Mason glimpsed a wound on the teen's back as he approached. He did not know what was wrong with the kid but it looked a lot like the other injured man. *Something fucked up is going on here*, he thought. He stopped at the side of the woman. He was not sure how to remove the teen without hurting the woman as well. The frustration lasted only a quarter of a second however it seemed an eternity of helplessness. The teen looked up and roared a hungry sound. Mason was out of patience. The uplifted head of the teen presented a perfect target. He swung his heavy foot at the thing's face. The motorcycle boots he wore were armored to protect one's legs from the weight of a 500 pound dirt bike. In this case, Mason's reinforced footwear became a sledgehammer. The teen reeled back several feet, bits of wet flesh flying from its mouth. Mason stepped over the woman and placed himself between her and the flailing teen. It rose to its feet and charged. Mason delivered a textbook perfect front kick to his attacker's sternum. Between the momentum of the rushing boy and the direct focused strike from Mason's boot, a tremendous amount of force was generated. Mason heard the boy's chest crack in several places as it flew backwards. The feel of the impact was unreal and disturbing. Chests were not supposed to be squishy.

"Get her up," Mason said; his eyes trained on the teen.

Tony turned and threw the small first aid kit to Veronica as she approached, freeing his hands to pick up the woman.

"Wait," said Veronica opening the first aid kit. She bent down and removed a large gauze bandage. Tearing open the olive drab plastic with her teeth, she expertly unwound the dressing. Looking in the case again she located a packet of antiseptic that looked like a green drive through ketchup packet.

"What the hell is going on?" Tony asked at Mason's side.

"I don't know man," Mason was sure the teen's chest was caved in, yet he still moved, slowly trying to get back to his feet.

"Did you bring your gun?" Mason asked.

"Locked in your glove box," Tony said feeling tense that the situation now warranted his pistol. The teen managed once more to gain a vertical base, standing, it lunged again. Nikki screamed. Not wanting to get too close, Mason struck it directly under the chin with his boot. The creature fell back hard, hitting it's head on the pavement. It appeared to be out cold.

"Why was he biting her?" Nikki asked trembling. Tony turned and looked at the woman. With all the excitement Tony had yet to absorb the reality of what he saw. It did not seem possible that the teen was biting the woman so his mind told him that he had just witnessed some bizarre attack.

"Biting?" Tony questioned. Veronica, having applied the antiseptic, cast the package aside. She looked up and nodded. Mason knew what he had seen was true, unlikely as all hell but he trusted his eyes.

"Look at him," Mason said. Tony stepped forward. Mason's arm caught him across the chest, "from here," he chided.

The teen was missing a small part of his left cheek and two fingers from his right hand. Most of the skin and some muscle from his left shoulder appeared to have been torn away. The neck was mostly intact but his collarbone was exposed through his shredded and bloody shirt.

A loud crash sounded from up the road, followed by tires squealing on pavement and another metal bending impact. The men could see a commotion in the distance near the office.

"Okay, what now?" Tony asked having seen enough.

"Get to the truck, my sword and your gun and get this woman to a hospital," Mason said thinking out loud.

"She's ready," Veronica said giving the gauze one last knot. Tony bent down and picked up the unconscious woman in a fireman's carry. Mason took one last look at the decaying teen and saw it begin to stir.

"Let's go," urged Nikki ten paces in front of the party.

Twenty Three

Nikki was the first to enter the camp at her top speed. She jumped into the cab of Jack's white Chevy. Veronica was the next to enter followed by Tony carrying the injured woman and finally Mason.

"Put her on the tailgate," Veronica said leading Tony to the rear of the truck. She pushed back a large ice chest clearing a space for the woman.

"Grab my sleeping bag," Tony said to Mason.

Mason moved around to Tony's tent, pulling the sleeping bag out like a magician revealing some trick. The bag flew open and unzipped. Mason laid out the sleeping bag on the bed of the truck and retrieved his sword. Tony bent down allowing the woman's bottom to rest on the tailgate in a seated position. He leaned her over gently on her uninjured side. Veronica took over and checked for a pulse. The woman burned with fever. Veronica jumped into the truck bed and opened the ice chest finding it full of cold drinks. She reached in and grabbed three cans of beer and placed them underneath the woman's neck and in her armpits. Veronica plunged her hands into the ice, retrieving two handfuls and rubbed the cubes over the woman's face.

Tony sprinted to the passenger's side of the truck and opened the door frightening Nikki. He reached in to the glove compartment but found it locked. Looking at the ignition his heart sank. The electrical system was engaged but there was no music to be heard. Reaching over Nikki's legs he turned the dial on the CD player. The dial was set to ON.

"Shit!" he exclaimed, dashing around the front of the vehicle. Mason hearing Tony's outburst, stripped the scabbard from his sword and ran to the front of the truck. He saw Tony leap into the driver's side and turn the starter. Nothing happened.

"Close that door," he said to Nikki as he shut his own door. He reached out and turned the CD player's switch off hoping that there might be enough remaining power to turn the motor. Nikki did not understand what he was doing and her fear seemed to double. He prayed in his head without words and turned the key. Silence once again. He opened the door and looked at his friend. Jack wore an expression that Tony had never seen before. He thought Mason was going to slug him.

"Dead," Tony said. Gunshots from the main campground area broke the moment. Nikki flinched and let out a small gasp.

"The bikes," Mason said in a flood of inspiration. He turned and ran to the trailer that held the men's motorcycles. Tony pulled the keys from the ignition and leaned over Nikki's lap. He knew she was terrified but *first things first*, he thought. Opening the glove compartment he pulled free his .380 caliber handgun, two full magazines and a single loose round. Leaning up and off of Nikki, he chambered the single bullet and slid a clip of six more into the grip of the weapon. He turned to the young blonde.

"Look, everything is going to be all right. You're with good people and we will do everything we can to keep you safe." He felt a little cheesy but thought that the girl needed to hear something positive. He switched his gun to his left hand and put his right on her shoulder squeezing gently for reassurance. She looked at him with her arms crossed as if she were holding herself and nodded.

"What about that woman?" Tony called out to Mason exiting the truck. Jack leaned his Kawasaki against the picnic table with a look of concern. *Could we ride three to a bike?* He did not think it would be possible. He was the better rider out of the two of them with more experience. That would mean Nikki in front of him and Veronica in back. *A Jack sandwich*, he thought. The seat on his bike was large enough, however the added weight would be difficult to control. Tony could take the injured woman but being unconscious, they would have to tie her hands around his waist. *No, that was a recipe for disaster*, he realized. *If the woman fell, Tony would be dragged down with her.*

"I don't know," Jack said disheartened.

"There is no need to worry about it," a quiet voice said. The voice belonged to Veronica. She eased herself off the back of the truck and pulled the edge of the sleeping bag over the woman's face. Nikki left the cab of the truck approaching the rear with hesitation.

"Is she…" Nikki's voice trailed off.

"Dead," said Veronica closing her eyes and saying a silent prayer.

118

Twenty Four

Zeke rolled his window down and projected a quarter cup of tobacco spit out of his mouth. The brown syrupy fluid dropped in the ebb and flow of the lake shore, seeming to want to stay together. The blob of liquid lip cancer rocked back and forth in the water, struggling to remain cohesive against the tide.

"Roll your window up, stupid!" Josh said holding his bitten arm. He had tied a dirty bandanna around the small wound. His young attacker had little teeth, but they were sharp. Josh had lost a silver dollar sized bit of skin. He reached his wounded arm over Zeke and pushed down on his already engaged door lock, just to be sure.

"There, see, that one is biting her," Lance said pointing. He and his two cronies sat in the idling silver Dodge watching the campground chaos as if it were a drive in movie.

"We should help them," Zeke protested.

"Be my guest," Lance said, a hint of laughter followed. He had loaded five 12 gauge rounds into the shotgun while watching the camp. Pumping the weapon, he chambered a round, ready to fire and loaded a final shell in the bottom. Josh watched silently holding his bitten arm.

"What are we going to do then?" Josh asked.

"Drive up past the old mine and back down," Lance answered as he switched the shotgun to safety and set it on the dash. He moved the gear lever to drive. The Dodge accelerated with indifference down the shore parallel to the water.

Andy was scared. The phone was dead and the lights were off. He heard roars and screams from outside. He really did not want to hide out and hope that the seven officers from town made it up in time to save him. The thought struck him as funny. *Seven cops for the town and maybe twenty Sheriffs for this part of the county.* No, it would be up to him to get out of this. *And the girl,* he thought, *yeah, I have to help her too.* The thought encouraged him. He would be responsible for her now. The camp gate was very close. Cars could not pass through the wreckage but he and the girl could. Hell, he would carry her if he had to.

"We have to get out of here," he said.

The girl looked up through tears of terror.

"We just have to go through the trees a little bit and we can move around the cars. Can you run?"

"Y…Yes," she stammered.

He helped her to her feet and picked up the fire extinguisher. Andy looked out the door glass, seeing no one in the immediate vicinity. He unlocked the door with his left hand and pushed it open. The horrible sounds of suffering increased in volume making the girl stiffen. Moving his large frame outside and holding the door with his back, he reached out and took the girl's small hand in his.

"Come on, follow me," he whispered.

Twenty Five

Mason stood next to Veronica looking out over the greater campground. He had dressed in his combat gear. After affixing his knife to its place on the harness he removed a pair of small field glasses from a pack.

"Things are falling apart out there," he said.

"I do not understand what is going on."

Mason lifted his mini binoculars to his eyes and spied the gate. He observed the twisted mass of cars and a small fire from the rear of a Honda.

"We are not making it through there, not exposed on the bikes, past all those lunatics." Mason saw a silver Dodge race up the camp road in the opposite direction. It passed their camp and continued up the hill.

"Where is he going?" Mason wondered aloud.

Veronica turned disappointed. She saw Nikki looking at the body of the woman.

"Nikki, where does this road go?"

Nikki turned startled. After a moment she answered Veronica.

"Up the mountain, really far then back down, I think." She turned to look at the body again but continued, "I have seen the Ranger come from that way before."

That was good enough for Tony. He stood in his motorcycle boots, camouflage pants, black t-shirt, full combat harness and his Sigarms .380 pistol in its holster.

"Sounds good to me," Tony said adjusting the fit of his gear.

"Okay, we are going for a ride, doesn't matter where, just out of here. Anything that can be used comes with us, mostly food and water," said Mason as he strapped his sword across his back.

Nikki stared at the woman underneath the sleeping bag. She had never seen a dead body before. She found it very strange that she was looking at the form of a person yet it was no longer breathing. She remembered the woman being attacked, falling down, and then Tony carrying her back to camp. The woman was alive five minutes ago and now, her body was empty.

"You doing alright?" Tony asked touching her shoulder.

Nikki snapped back to reality and felt like she was going to cry. She could not allow herself to fall apart in front of the others. She told herself to be strong and breathed unsteady breaths.

"Not really," she said louder than she realized. Veronica noticed Nikki's condition. She knew that if a person had a job to do they could get their mind off of dire circumstances. Her father had asked Veronica to help with the injured during the earthquake. The action of assisting him distracted her, preventing the young girl from breaking down.

"Nikki, I need your help," Veronica said holding a backpack open on the picnic table.

Nikki turned to Veronica and screamed. Over Veronica's shoulder, from the camp road she could see the teen creature approaching.

"We got company!" Tony hollered drawing his pistol. Mason unsheathed his sword and held it high. Veronica swung up Tony's paint gun from the table, looked at it for a moment and found the safety. She switched the air rifle to fire and aimed at the teen.

"Get Behind me!" Mason said to Veronica. She moved fast, Nikki stood frightened behind Tony.

The thing moved in an almost comical manner. It jerked and swayed with strange rhythm. Now twenty feet away it raised its arms and bellowed a greedy cry.

"Do I shoot him?" Tony asked in unsure horror.

Mason was thinking the same thing. All his life he had known quite a bit about how to hurt people. He had studied the sword, martial arts and war games but he never wanted to actually use what he knew. Fights were fine but this was getting too serious. He had already devastated the kid's chest. Whatever was wrong with the teen was not curable.

"Shoot!" Mason said.

Tony hesitated; he did not want to go to jail for murder but there was no other choice. He considered a warning shot. The thought instantly evaporated with a roar from the teen.

"Does everyone agree that this is self defense?" Tony asked with urgency.

"Yes!" yelled Veronica, Nikki was speechless.

The trigger seemed to weigh a ton. It would not move. Feeling stupid for forgetting, he thumbed the safety off, braced the weapon in both hands and fired. The round hit the teen creature directly in the chest. A small thick drip of dark blood trickled out of the hole, more exiting the thing's back. The creature was pushed back by the bullet but remained on its feet. Nikki, whose head was hidden behind Tony, was the only one not to see the impact. Tony was a good shot, especially at ten paces; he hit the creature center mass, right through the heart.

"What the fuck?" Mason said as he lowered his center of gravity into something his old Sensei called a *cat stance*. The walking corpse steadied itself and looked at the dumbstruck Tony. The creature started forward once again. Mason became amazed in a very dark way at the sight. What he had just witnessed was not possible and that frightened him very much. The fear granted Mason a sort of strength and sureness that he now knew what he had to do.

"Hey, over here," Mason said to the creature. It jerked its head in his direction and its shoulders followed. Mason dropped his full weight on to his front leg and swung his sword with all of his might. He was surprised at how easily the sharpened steel blade went through the teen's neck. Correcting his balance after the stroke, he realized that he used more force than needed. The teen's damaged body fell to the earth empty and still.

Mason was shaken. They all were. Nikki finally looked around Tony and saw the teen's headless body. She held back a scream, choosing instead to hold on to Tony's arm. Her touch would have been pleasing to Tony if the situation was different. Now he stood, nearly frozen with both hands on his pistol. He lowered the weapon and thumbed the safety back on, struggling to keep his thoughts together.

Veronica held herself motionless; every muscle that she owned tense to the brink of shivering. She saw the thing's head roll with a heavy rumble in front of her. It stopped on its side, the jaw still opening and closing slightly. *Left over nerve energy,* she attempted to reassure herself. In all her years of studying medicine and the physical sciences she had learned much about the human body. What she had just witnessed was impossible; never the less it was happening. As she stared at the head she almost screamed at what she saw. The thing's eyes were looking directly at her. *No,* she thought doubtful, *it is not possible.* She moved to her right near the truck and the dried orbs in their sunken sockets followed her.

"The head," she said in a breathless voice, pointing with the paint gun.

Mason, still clutching his sword moved in closer for a look. He stopped at the body and stepped his foot on it to make sure it did not get back up. Tony and Nikki approached in hesitation. The undead eyes turned to Tony as the jaw opened once more. Tony made a feminine sound of surprise.

"Why is it doing that?" Mason asked, his deep voice wavering.

"It is not supposed to do that," Veronica said more to herself than the others.

"It's not dead," cried Nikki. Another burst of gunfire sounded from the campground. Mason reacted by looking back. The fire at the gate had grown. Smoke began to thicken over the far off campgrounds. He saw two men running towards jet skis chased by another. *Good luck guys,* he thought. Turning back, he stepped off the body and gave the head a hard kick, sending the heavy mass past the truck into the brush. Mason's eyes met Veronica's, they said nothing. The camp was silent save for the distant clamor of chaos.

A solid thump sounded from the rear of the truck. Veronica noticed the vehicle move upward at her side as if someone had jumped out. *Oh no*, she thought as her hand squeezed hard onto the grip of the paint gun. Slowly they all turned in anticipation. Nikki's position gave her the best view. She saw the sleeping bag now on the ground; it began to move. It gasped a labored inhale. The fabric of the bag stirred, exposing a woman's leg. The dead woman struggled to her feet, dark slime oozing from the wound on her back. The standing corpse turned, opened its mouth, and started towards Nikki.

Veronica fired three paintball rounds at the dead woman's face. The first burst the woman's unprotected right eye in a splash of blue paint and aqueous jelly. The second flattened on the brow of her left, dripping its thick hue over her last good eye. The third round whizzed off into the distance missing its target. Veronica's movement spurred the men into action. Mason pulled Veronica backwards out of the isle created by the bench and his truck. He took her place, not wanting her to be in such a vulnerable spot. Tony lifted his gun and stepped in front of Nikki. He switched the gun to fire.

The dead woman raged sightless with her arms outstretched. Without direction, she moved about the campground grasping at the air. Tony backed Nikki towards the truck clearing a space for the thrashing creature.

"She is blind," Veronica said.

The woman reacted to the sound, violently moving towards Veronica's voice. It smashed an already bloody knee into the bench, almost tumbling over. Mason waved his sword in the air to catch the others attention with his finger to his lips in a Shush gesture. The dead woman clawed about the air without vision, her jaw grinding open and closed with a horrible single minded purpose.

Nikki no longer hid behind Tony. He was in front of her, sure to keep himself between her and the creature. For some reason that she did not understand, she had grown bolder. She could not believe what she was seeing. She had just been looking at the woman's dead body and now, it was up, walking around, trying to bite them. She was still very afraid, but immersed in a sensation of unreality that made her a little curious. The woman-thing remained ten paces from Tony, still near the bench. It lifted its blind and damaged face while apparently sniffing the air. Moving its head as if it could see Tony it began to approach him. Nikki's attention was caught once again by the glimmer of Mason's waving sword.

Still silent and using an improvised sort of sign language, Mason looked to Tony while making the shape of a gun with his left hand. He pointed the finger gun to his head and moved his thumb. Tony pointed at the headless body with his left hand and made a face as if to say, *I shot that one and it didn't work.* Mason appeared frustrated with Tony. He tapped two fingers on his forehead, indicating a shot to the head. Nikki saw Tony's shoulders slump at Mason's nonverbal suggestion.

Tony did not want to shoot the woman. He had already shot someone today and he was not feeling good about it. As the woman drew closer, he lifted his arms, braced himself and took aim. The stress of the day was beginning to wear on Tony. He had the dead woman in his sights yet he pulled the trigger with his eyes closed. He knew it was safe enough at such close range. He would hit the target however he had no desire to see her head come apart. His fearful imagination had betrayed him. Instead of her skull exploding in a disgusting hail of blood and water soluble paint, his weapon punched a neat hole just above the bridge of her nose. He did not see how she died for the second time. He only heard the woman's body slump to the ground empty of whatever hellish element that had animated it. Tony opened his eyes.

"Let's go, now!" Mason said, his voice seeming to boom in the stillness. Tony and Nikki stood transfixed on the body of the twice dead young woman.

Veronica dropped the paint rifle on the bench. She picked up the backpack and removed the clothes inside, setting them on the table. Mason rummaged through the clothes and produced a yellow and white motorcycle jersey. He spied one quick look at Veronica's tight smooth stomach before he spoke.

"Do you want to wear this?" he asked offering her the jersey.

With all the mayhem she had completely forgotten that she had used her shirt to try and stop the man's bleeding. She had been running around for what seemed like hours in only her sports bra. Despite the horrible fear and urgent need to get moving, Veronica blushed again. She took the shirt and nodded in gratitude. She quickly pulled it on. It was large on her. It smelled different like all borrowed clothes do. This smell was not due only to a difference in washing detergents. It did smell clean, but it also smelled like Jack. The scent was masculine. Veronica found herself lingering on the aroma for a moment. She cast off the thought and took the backpack to the rear of the truck. Kicking aside the sleeping bag at her feet, she reached in and caught the ice chest with an outstretched hand.

Nikki tapped Tony on the shoulder. He turned. She had a very sour look on her face as if she were about to cry. He looked at her with understanding and tried to put on a brave face. His consoling smile comforted her. He took her by the shoulder and walked her to his bike. Tony grabbed what looked like plastic armor off his leaning motorcycle. The shoulder pads were white and red, strewn with many stickers and a few abrasions which Nikki assumed were from crashes. She hoped that Tony knew how to ride his motorcycle well.

"Lift up your arms," he said holding the chest protector above her. She complied. He noticed how her full breasts lifted as well. *Not now,* he thought to himself, *Yikes!*

"This is going to protect you if we have a little accident," he continued pulling the hardened plastic gear over her arms, her head popping through the top of the armor.

"It is designed for my size but will help you if we go down. That won't happen, this is just in case. You have to hold on tight to me and kind of lean to the same sides that I lean while we go around corners."

"I have never ridden on a motorcycle before," she said quietly almost embarrassed.

"Piece of cake, I won't let you down," he reassured with a small smile.

Veronica finished placing seven small bottles of water in the backpack. Looking for more in the ice chest she found only four Cokes and a large number of beers. Mason having just attached his paint gun to his handlebars with duct tape, approached.

"Did you guys bring enough beer?" Veronica asked frustrated.

"Bring whatever can fit, its better to have more than less," he answered shrugging. Veronica packed in the cokes and two beers. Zipping up the backpack, she jumped out of the truck.

"What about food?" Veronica asked Jack.

"Right here."

On the table before Jack were two brown paper bags full of canned goods. Spaghetti and meatballs, chili beans, small cans of Salmon and a half full box of chocolate flavored protein bars.

"Fine dining," she said.

Mason produced another larger backpack that still had a few items within. He began to pack some of the food inside.

"We have a few steaks and other stuff in a different ice chest but I don't want to bring any meat with us," he said watching her reaction.

"You saw that too?" she asked.

"Yeah, it was like she was trying to catch our scent. She was blind, but she still knew where Tony was."

Veronica looked at Mason with a serious expression. An explosion sounded at the camp gate. A gas tank in one of the cars had given away to the fire. The party flinched yet with everything they had been through so far, the reaction was almost subdued.

"Put my gear on," said Mason.

Veronica nodded with a tired exhale and went to the motorcycle.

Tony looked at Nikki. In his plastic armor, black gloves and black helmet, everything far too big for her, she looked like a little elfin warrior. Mason handed Tony his paint gun and a roll of duct tape. Tony taped the rifle to the handlebars without a question. He knew what to do without thinking about it. Mason lifted a backpack to Nikki and helped her put it on over her chest protector. He bent down, adjusted the front straps and pulled it snug on her over burdened body. Jack could see the fear in her eyes through the open visor of the helmet. He put his hands on her shoulders and smiled at her hoping to bring some measure of assurance. She swayed underneath the weight of her equipment.

"I'll give you a hand' he said nodding. She nodded back, her helmet moving in an exaggerated bobble.

Tony mounted his yellow Yamaha allowing his weight to push the seat lower. Jack helped Nikki get on the back. He steadied her while Tony threw two hard kicks on the starter. The Yamaha roared to life with a loud sputtering rumble. Tony settled in as Nikki squeezed her arms around his midsection. He patted her locked hands in tender reassurance.

Veronica stood waiting in Jack's protective gear. She pulled on the larger of the backpacks and looked out over the camp. An assembly of creatures noticed the clamor of Tony's bike. They staggered in her direction. Mason started his bike on the first kick. Still looking out at the greater camping area, she watched more of what used to be people, head towards their camp. The specters shambled and shuffled forward gaining ground on their position. Seven or eight creatures reached the road very near as Veronica mounted the back of Mason's cycle. As the bikes pulled out, she saw a dead body in the distance, sit up and look in her direction.

Twenty Six

The silver Dodge climbed up the mountain road. All terrain tires held fast to the earth while the truck's suspension compressed and flexed to absorb the uneven surface. Lance knew that he was driving too fast. Fear and disbelief had settled in his heart where once sat a macabre amusement. People were dying. He was not dying, and that is all that ever mattered to Lance. He was content to watch the situation unfold and witness psychotic people attack each other. Then, somewhere in the back of his self absorbed mind, his inner sociopath gave way to the voice of reason. As the situation worsened at the campground, he became very afraid. A fear, the likes of which, the spoiled young man had never known in his privileged life.

The trail road was wide and crossed with deep sun baked ruts. Lance and Zeke had their seat belts strapped firm, but Josh, sitting in the middle had no such restraints. Josh was growing feverish. The rocking of the dirt road jostled him to and fro, making the man feel deathly ill.

"Roll down the window man," Josh pleaded as he rag dolled around in the cab. He was very hot, his fever boiling.

Lance thought the camp must be miles behind them by now. He slowed the vehicle and cranked down his window. Zeke rolled his window down quickly and spit out a huge wad of tobacco and spit. He was so overcome with fear. Fear of the people at the camp, but more so a fear of Lance yelling at him, if he rolled the window down without permission. He had been suffering with the wad of tobacco in his mouth for the better part of twenty minutes. The bumpy ride had forced some of the grim fluid down his throat which he swallowed without complaint. There was a greenish tinge on his face as he poked his head out of the moving vehicle to clear the remnants from his gums. Zeke thought he was going to vomit.

Going slower now, the truck had ceased its violent rocking. Josh was tired. He leaned back and decided to get some shut eye. His arm throbbed gently in time with each breath. He thought to himself that he would rest for a little bit; *just a little bit*. Lance's fear returned. *What if what made the people crazy was in the air?* his paranoia wondered.

"That's enough air, roll 'em back up," he ordered.

It seemed like they had been walking for hours. Andy Walters still held on to the girl's hand. Her bare feet were dirty from walking on the asphalt. He wished that he could offer her his shoes but they would not have come close to fitting her. She was small, maybe sixteen and only dressed in a pink one piece bathing suit. He worried about her exposure to the elements and would have liked to give her his shirt. His modesty prevented him from offering. They did not see any one else make it out of the campground. The girl ran for a solid ten minutes once they cleared the gate. Andy had to reassure her that they were far enough away to convince her to slow down. He needed to rest after their escape. Now they walked.

"What's your name?" he asked.

She looked up at him speechless. He could see her ear was crusted over with dried blood. He leaned down pulling her to a stop. She tried to keep walking but did not want to let go of his hand.

"Let me see your ear."

She pulled her head away with a flinch. He put his hand on her shoulder to hold her in place.

"I won't touch it, I just want to see."

Turning her body Andy saw that the top of her ear was missing. A crescent shaped curve of tattered skin gave hint to teeth marks. The surface of the wound had dried and the ear underneath towards her cheek looked bruised. The girl had a dazed look in her eyes. He took his hand from her shoulder and felt her forehead; she flinched again but submitted. She was running a fever.

"How are you feeling?" he asked.

Down the shady mountain road came an ambulance. Andy turned to look and saw the red lights flash a greeting. The girl saw the vehicle approach and grew faint with relief.

"We are going to be okay," he smiled. Andy stood and waved the ambulance down.

"I wonder if anyone made it out of there okay," Zeke said. Lance did not care. He was glad that Wanda left before the problems began but only in as much as his car was safely out of the camp. He loved that car more than he cared for Wanda. Then he remembered the blood on her towel at camp. *No*, he thought, *that was just a coincidence. She started her period and split because she was dripping all over her favorite big bottomed bathing suit.* He was sure that must be what happened. Whatever was the case, he was out of harm's way now. When he got back to town he would tell everyone how he had only been able to save Josh and Zeke. He would frame the facts to show how heroic he was; saving Josh from the little demon and waiting for Zeke to jump in the truck. His men would go along with his version of events; they always did.

"How long we been on the road?" asked Zeke.

"Hour or so, I don't know," Lance answered annoyed.

Josh slumped lifelessly against Zeke.

The road ahead narrowed around a curve. Lance accelerated around the corner as Josh stirred. He lifted his head, opened his eyes with a slight flutter.

"How ya feeling partner?" asked Zeke to the waking Josh.

Josh turned his head mechanically towards Zeke, his jaw slack and open. Roaring with hunger, Josh grasped at Zeke who withdrew screaming. Startled and panicked, Lance turned his body towards his passengers. His flight response forced Lance to step down hard on the gas, plunging the truck over the edge of the dirt road.

Falling and bouncing down the overgrown dried grass hill, Lance absent mindedly tried to hit his breaks. The vehicle only intermittently made contact with the ground as it fell. The anti-lock breaks would not allow the wheels to come to a complete stop. Lance was lucky, for if the wheels did lock up, the inertia of the large truck would have caused it to tumble end over end. The shotgun bounced about the cab, its butt end knocking Lance on the right cheekbone. Zeke's screams were constant and pitiful.

The ground began to level underneath the truck. It came to a rapid stop, slamming the front left wheel into a small gully, shattering the shocks. The airbags deployed saving Lance from crushing his chest against the steering wheel. Lance was in a panic. As the airbags deflated he could still hear growls and pleas for mercy. He felt around and popped open his seatbelt. Jumping from the leaning truck, he saw the stock of his shotgun on the seat. He reached in fast, snatching up the weapon to the sounds of guttural roars. Lance switched off the safety and fired the shotgun directly into the cab, pumped it and fired again, and again. Three rounds of triple aught buckshot devastated any matter within the vehicle. Windows, leather seats, clothing and human tissue were shredded and blended together in a frenzy of careless fear. The blasts echoed against the limestone walls of the mountain, diminished, then silenced.

    Lance turned, closed his door and slid down with his back against his truck to sit on the ground. He held his shotgun close and checked to see if it had a live round chambered.

    "What now?" he said aloud. Looking to his right he saw the broken shock absorber hanging from its truss. Knowing that he would have to walk from now on, he stood. Lance's father had taught him to be a survivor; to go through anything and anyone to succeed. Lance was going to do just that, no matter the cost.

    He walked around the other side of the truck and opened the door. A tangled mass that was once Zeke fell halfway out. The top of his seat belt was sheared off by the shotgun blasts with the bottom portion remaining in place. Gravity took hold and the belt slowly unraveled allowing Zeke's nettled corpse to slip to the ground. Lance stepped back, tracking the body's fall with the end of his weapon. He needed to retrieve the rest of his shotgun shells despite his fear. Once he was sure that Zeke was not going to get up, he looked in the cab. Half of Josh's face was missing. There was still some cheekbone, the edge of the right ear and part of the right eye, but everything else was sheared off. Lance actually spent a moment feeling sorry for Josh. He looked down to Josh's arm. The bandanna had torn free revealing congealed dark green foam surrounding the wound. Lance looked back at the slumped, bloody mess that was Zeke. There was no greenish tint to any of his bright red blood. A connection formed in Lance's inarticulate mind. Josh was sick but Zeke was okay. He probably did not have to shoot them both.

"Hmm, that is weird," he mumbled. Reaching down to the passenger's floorboard he retrieved the box of twelve gauge shells. He opened the lid and saw that it contained six more shells. Closing the door, he walked away from the grim scene to the back of his truck. Opening the tailgate he looked in to see if there was anything he might be able to use. His ice chest and other equipment had been left back at the camp. Sitting on the tailgate he proceeded to load three more rounds into his shotgun. He ejected the top round to make sure once again that a live shell was in the chamber ready to go. Loading the ejected round back in the bottom of the weapon, the thought finally occurred to Lance that he had just killed Zeke. He turned his head to see Zeke's torn body piled upon the earth in an impossible contortion. Lance's expression was not one of sorrow or remorse but rather a look of concern for himself. He worried for a moment what might happen if the police took a close look at his truck. If he had fired only once he could pretend it was an accident. Any flatfoot could tell that there was more than one round fired. Looking out over the dried grass of the hill he resolved that he would deal with that possibility later. He would claim self defense and that he was in mortal fear for his life. That part was true at least.

A high whine from the dirt road broke the silence. It was an approaching motorcycle. *No,* he thought as the sound increased, *more than one.* The sound jerked and rumbled on the road above his location. He was too low to see the surface of the road or who was on the bikes. Lance dropped to his feet off the uneven tailgate and ran towards the road. The grade was steep and the road further away than he thought. Halfway up the rise he noticed the pitch of the motors shift down. They had passed him. As the sound diminished he finally made his way onto the road. He grunted in anger at his timing. A minute faster and he could have talked some poor sap into giving him a ride. He decided that if anyone else came along on the road, he would be there to greet them. They would give him a ride back, one way or another. He did have a shotgun after all.

Disappointed but determined to get back to his town, Lance began walking up the road with his shotgun safety off.

Twenty Seven

Jack Mason had lived an adventurous life. He had seen and done some pretty strange things in his thirty years. He considered himself lucky to be alive in some regards. He had witnessed a couple of knife fights, participated in brawls, had guns in his face, been arrested, been hit by cars and even spent some time in his youth experimenting with drugs. All the weird things that had ever happened to him in his past were nothing compared to this day. As he steered the Kawasaki up the mountain, careful to avoid the many rivulets in the earth, he considered what he had seen. There was no way to explain how a person could die and get back up. *It just doesn't happen*, he thought. He recalled how sick it felt to kick the teen in the chest with his full force. In Kempo class as a kid he was able to break three, one inch pine boards with his bare foot. Combined with the weight of his reinforced boot, he was sure he had shattered the kid's chest, yet he kept on coming. He did not want to hurt the boy but Mason saw no alternative. He wanted to pull the bike over and talk to the others. He wanted confirmation that what he had just seen had indeed happened. They had been proceeding at a good pace for what felt like an hour, they must be far enough away by now.

Nikki held on for dear life. Her arms were clamped around Tony with her face buried in his back. She had her head turned towards the mountainside to avoid looking out over the vast valley below. She was not afraid of heights but the rough road and previous terrors had left her squeamish. Tony's helmet was too large for her. It was padded and blocked some of the noise of the motorcycle but slid about on her head. Behind the closed tinted visor, it almost felt roomy. As the tree strewn limestone rolled by, in the confines of her helmet, she wept. Tears flowed down her cheeks within the protective chamber. She squeezed Tony to steady herself on the bike, but also to for reassurance that she was not alone. She did not want to think about the things that she had seen. She wanted to get home and see her parents. She did not always get along with her folks, yet could not help but miss them now. Her tears ran faster at the thought. A bump in the road sent her body flying upward. She held fast to Tony and stayed on the seat. It was very strange to her that she was holding on so tightly to a man she did not know. She remembered how he made sure to stay in front of her when the things were around. Nikki was too afraid at the time to realize it, but she might not be alive if not for the actions of these men. They were good people. With the distance between her and the camp growing, she started to feel just a little bit safe.

Veronica wanted answers. She read biology and medical textbooks in her spare time for relaxation. Never in any of her studies had she ever come across any reference to any sort of condition that could be behind the events she had just witnessed. As she jostled about on the back of Jack's motorcycle, her body used its natural sense of balance, gained through years of ballet as a child, to steady herself. She did so without mental effort giving her much needed time to sort her thoughts. There was no explanation for what she had seen. Chemicals, nerve agents, or even drugs could make a normal person insane to the point of violence. PCP could release almost superhuman strength along with unexplainable behavior. Yet there was no compound that could allow the human body to withstand a bullet to the chest and survive. She considered the teen's severed head. Leftover charges in the nervous system could cause twitching and random movement. She knew in her heart that there was nothing random about the eyes. The head's eyes did indeed track her movement. They followed her with a purpose. *How in the physical world was it possible?* she questioned.

Veronica had seen to the woman; observed the fever progress faster than she knew was possible. The woman did not die from blood loss, she was sure of that. Veronica thought it might be possible that the woman expired from shock or some other internal problem that would not be evident from a quick examination; *a bad heart perhaps*. The number of questions was overwhelming and no good explanations came to her mind. She was not yet a doctor and should not expect herself to have all the answers. Uncertainties and impossibilities stood in the way of her understanding, frightening Veronica deeply.

Tony fought with the handlebars to keep the motorcycle under control. Jack had always been the better rider and now Tony was attempting to keep up. He felt Nikki's arms, like a vice, holding onto his midsection. He wished he was in better shape. The girl was close and even though he flexed his stomach muscles while riding, there was the soft cushion of beer fat between her arms and his abdominals. He would have felt worse about his conditioning were it not for the dire circumstances that they were running from. The motorcycles had helped the party escape the campground but Tony still feared the possibility of running into more lunatics. This was unfamiliar country and he had no idea exactly where they were headed. They had no choice but to take the mountain road out of danger. Tony hoped that the worst was over. The thought that there may be more wild freaks running around was disconcerting. He took a mental inventory of his weapons. He had five rounds in his pistol and one extra magazine with six bullets. He wished that he had brought a box of fifty or even his old twenty two caliber rifle. *Wishing can't help now*, he thought, eleven rounds, a knife and a paint gun was all he had. He wished he had been more prepared for trouble, but who could have foreseen this day? Tony promised himself that once he got home he would buy a new gun and a case of bullets. *Some sit ups might be a good idea too*, he thought as Nikki's arms squeezed him even tighter.

    The road had been a constant back and forth from steep grade to small area of level ground than back to an upwards climb for what seemed like over an hour. Emerging at the top of a hill, Jack saw that the road ahead was flat for some distance. He could tell from the surrounding geography that they were not at the top of the range yet but they had come to a stretch of level ground. Climbing hills, even without a passenger, is difficult work. Balancing, shifting gears, and avoiding rutted terrain, requires a whole body effort. Slowing up, he sat down into his seat and relaxed as much as he could while maintaining a steady pace.

    They entered a small valley with tress extending much needed shade from both sides of the road. The sun flecked bright patches through the canopy making the ride seem almost peaceful. Jack spied a structure in the distance. Pulling in his clutch he nudged his foot shifter into second but held the lever, allowing him to coast. Tony glided forward to Jack's right and matched his speed. They both saw the small structure in an open clearing. It appeared to be a prefab kit shack. It was sturdy but had seen better days. Tony motioned with a nod in the shack's direction. Almost on cue, both men killed their engines and coasted in front of the shack. Holding his bike up with his left leg, Tony put his hand to his gun. For a nervous moment, they just stared at the door of the old shack. The frightened part of Tony's mind, the part that made him sleep with the light on until he was eight years old, expected a tattered monster to emerge flailing madly out the door. The large padlock on the outside securing the entrance gave him reassurance that no one was within.

"Anybody home," Jack called out, breaking the stillness.

Another tense moment of gentile silence gave way to the chatter of birds enjoying a carefree afternoon.

"Let's check it out," Jack said.

Twenty Eight

The lock was rusty from years of exposure. Three good bashes from the butt of Mason's combat knife knocked the shackle open. Tony stood with his weapon ready, pointing at the door. Mason pulled the door open as Tony moved in. Light slivered in through small gaps in the boards that made up the walls of the shack. Disturbed dust floated through the air turning the light into hard rays that bounced against the opposite wall. The plywood floor creaked underneath Tony's feet. The space measured about twelve by ten feet with the door on the long end. A heavy workbench sat at the far end of the room opposite the door. An array of excavation tools hung from a rack on the back wall containing two shovels, a pick axe a woodsman's axe, an oxidized machete as well as various hammers and tools. There was a dusty smell to the place but not a moldy one. Tony assumed that the floor was raised up on pallets or water resistant wood, to keep out the dampness during the rain. Two plastic milk crates on the floor held various rags and a pair of safety goggles. Mason appeared at the entrance with his motorcycle. He rolled it in, backwards so that the front end pointed towards the door.

"No need to let anyone know we are here," he said.

Tony stepped outside to get his bike. Nikki's head poked around the corner looking in.

Tony saw Veronica removing her backpack. She rotated her neck, stretching to relieve her tension. She looked down the road, back towards camp. She seemed to be deep in thought. Tony wheeled his bike towards the shack, stopping he asked,

"You doing all right?"

Turning, she exhaled loudly as if to say, *Hell no*.

"I think we need to talk about what we all just witnessed," Veronica said as she paced about in the middle of the shack. She was the only one standing. Nikki sat unencumbered on the workbench next to the pile of gear that she had removed from her person. Tony sat on an over turned milk crate next to Jack, who was leaning on his motorcycle seat. They all gave their attention to Veronica.

"I have been thinking and the most likely reason for those people's behavior is a disease," she continued. "It must be transferred in the blood, by exposure from a bite. The woman I treated had a fever that climbed faster than anything I have ever read about. Now that to me says disease. Some pathogen from the teen infected her."

"Are you sure she was dead?" Nikki asked slowly, almost struggling to get the words out. Veronica understood Nikki's disbelief and moved close to her.

"Nik, I am positive," she assured. "She was gone. I felt no heartbeat and her breathing stopped. I did compressions but decided against mouth to mouth because I did not have a micro mask for protection. I guess I suspected somehow that she was infected."

"I had that feeling too, but what kind of bug makes people want to chew on each other?" Jack questioned thinking about the man with the hole in his neck.

Veronica turned to Jack with a weary look.

"Nothing. I mean I have no idea; something no one has ever seen before," she said leaning her tired body against the workbench.

"I hit that dude right in the heart," Tony said, a touch of guilt in his voice. "When you get hit in the heart, your body shuts off, but he kept moving. And then the thing with the head," Tony lifted his hands in defense as if to say that he had enough.

"Yes, there was something else I noticed that was odd," Veronica said standing once again. "When you shot him, there was very little blood, granted his heart was most likely destroyed, so that makes sense, but the woman; she hardly bled at all from a head wound. There should have been more internal pressure, especially from the exit wound."

Veronica appeared to be thinking. She walked in silence, looking at the floor. Nikki lifted her tired head back and leaned it on the wall. Tony wanted to say something nice to Nikki but hesitated. Jack watched Veronica pace. He liked the thoroughness of her thinking. She spoke.

"Those people are dead," she said causing a jolt of adrenalin to fire inside Nikki's body. "They have no blood pressure so no heartbeat. That is why shooting one in the heart has little effect. However, sever or destroy the head and they stop. But what in God's name could do such a thing?"

"A chemical weapon?" Jack suggested.

Veronica considered for a moment.

"Those take effect on exposure by eating, drinking or breathing, not a bite. A biological weapon might be more likely but I really do not know."

She paced back to the workbench. Opening up a backpack she fished out a bottle of water. Noticing the pale look on Nikki's face she offered the bottle to the young blond. Nikki accepted it with only a nod.

"A bite is skin contact," Tony said.

Veronica shrugged.

"Yes, however that says to me infection, something along the lines of a disease. The woman was bitten by a carrier and became sick herself. If it were a chemical weapon why use it out up here, and who would want to?" she questioned, brushing her long hair away from her face.

"The government could be behind it," Jack said with a stern look, "They don't give a damn about anyone."

Veronica thought about the care her father had received compliments of the U.S. Army and felt a shudder. She gave Jack a knowing look of agreement.

Tony looked to Nikki, who seemed distant. *The girl's been though a lot*, he thought. He wished he could get up and reassure her that the worst was over. He wished he could reassure himself. Then his eyes fell to underneath the workbench. He saw a shape hanging from two hooks under the table; the unmistakable shape of a rifle.

"Wait a second…" Tony said approaching Nikki low. She reacted and withdrew her legs up onto the workbench. Crouched, Tony reached in underneath Nikki's butt, making her feel very vulnerable. She relaxed once she saw him produce an old rifle. Jack sprung to his feet and moved close for a better look. It was a single shot .410 gauge shotgun. A very small model with a thin barrel; the .410 was the kind of weapon a kid might get as their first gun. Tony broke open the breach to find the weapon unloaded. It was dirty but not rusty. Tony brushed away some of the dirt and found that it was only dust clinging to its well oiled surface. The men huddled over the weapon like mothers over a newborn child.

"A squirrel gun," Tony said. A small smile formed on Nikki's face as she saw the glee shared by the two men. *Boys*, she thought.

"Look for shells," Jack said.

For the next few moments the men searched the shack. Jack found an old red metal toolbox. Within he found a clear plastic bag, browned with age. Inside he could see a number of small shotgun rounds. Forgetting the other items in the toolbox he turned and held them up to show Tony.

"Got it," he said.

The decayed plastic bag disintegrated, dropping shells on the plywood floor. They rolled around in various circular paths. Both men scrambled and retrieved the shells. Veronica raised an eyebrow to Nikki while avoiding the rounds with her feet. She leaned again on the bench and drank some much needed water. Nikki, burdened by her fears, had forgotten about the water that Veronica had handed her. The shock of the day was wearing off a little and she realized that she was thirsty. She drank half the bottle in a single sip.

Nine green shotgun shells stood on their ends on a small corner of the workbench. Jack thought that there was something strange about the shells. They lacked a brand name printed on the side as he was accustomed to seeing. He picked up a shell and examined it closely.

"Are these home loads?" he asked himself.

"What kind?" Tony asked concerned. Jack thumbed at the top of the shotgun shell. The plastic crimping that held back the load opened easily. A small paper wad stood at the top of the shell. Removing the wad, he was disheartened to find the shell packed with a chunky white substance.

"It's rock salt," Jack said disappointed. "They're home loads of rock salt."

"What does that mean?" Veronica asked moving close to Jack. He put the round down on the workbench in disappointment.

"Instead of loading lead or steel ball bearings, you pack the shell with rock salt. It won't kill someone but it stings like hell. They are meant to scare people off," he explained as he moved back to his motorcycle.

Tony looked around the workbench. He smiled at Nikki quickly and began searching the toolbox. Screwdrivers, wrenches, and other tools one would expect to find within a toolbox were present. He found a metal container of nuts and bolts and another with assorted nails underneath the tool tray. He thought for a moment removing the nails and setting them aside.

"We can reload scrap into the shells," Tony said. Jack agreed with a nod. Veronica looked at Tony. .

"We dump out the salt and fill it with nails and bolts. They won't be as powerful as a real shell, but they will work," Tony elaborated for her.

Jack removed the gas cap from Tony's motorcycle. He looked in the tank, smelling the strangely pleasing odor of petroleum. There was close to half a tank remaining. Replacing the cap and looking at the semi opaque tank on his bike, he could tell that he had over three quarters of a tank left. This worried Jack.

"Did you have a full tank when we left?" Jack asked.

Tony turned from his searching and looked at Jack.

"Yeah, topped off before we left home."

Jack leaned against his bike and exhaled. He knew what was wrong. Tony's bike was twenty years old. It was heavy, over burdened by two riders and a backpack full of water. Mason's bike was two years old made from modern alloys with far better fuel efficiency. The lack of gas could be a problem.

"You're down to half a tank," Jack said. Shifting his gaze to Nikki he asked,

"How far is it back to town?"

Nikki finished the last of her water and looked at Jack not realizing that she had been asked a question; after a moment, it registered.

"Um, I dunno, we have to go pretty high up then back down. I have never been this way before," she said sorry for not having a better answer. Both men seemed very concerned.

"Why?" she asked realizing that she had to pee. Jack began.

"We have been riding for, what, an hour, maybe more. That means that Tony's bike has another hour worth of gas in it. If we can get to the top before then, he can coast down but if it's more than that," Jack shrugged and looked away.

"We end up walking," Tony finished for him.

"Then we walk," Veronica said, "We keep going. Jack can go ahead on his bike and get help if it comes to that, but we keep moving."

Jack liked the cut of her jib. He smiled at Veronica and nodded. The idea of walking frightened Nikki. She feared becoming lost in an unfamiliar forest at night. Her growing apprehension at such a possibility increased the pressure on her bladder. She slipped her legs down off the workbench, stood and looked at Veronica.

"Wanna go outside for a minute?" Nikki asked.

Veronica made a questioning face, failing to understand what Nikki wanted. Nikki mouthed the words, "I gotta pee," and Veronica understood.

"We are going out for a moment," Veronica said leading Nikki towards the door.

"Wait," Jack said, "Have you ever fired a gun?"

Veronica stopped in front of Jack, a half smile on her face.

"Yes. A thirty eight caliber, Smith and Wesson, Bodyguard; My father's gun" she answered hoping that she recited the gun's name correctly.

Jack smiled. *Oh yeah*, he thought, *this chick is cool.*

"Let her borrow your gun, man," he said to Tony. Tony looked at his gun as if he were going to miss it but agreed with Jack. He un-holstered the weapon, checked the safety and handed it to her. Veronica accepted the small pistol and held it with her finger off the trigger, pointing forward down the barrel.

"Thanks," she said to Jack. The two girls left the shack.

"Where are they going?" Tony inquired.

Jack rolled his eyes.

Twenty Nine

Veronica led the way to a thicket of trees twenty yards behind the shack.

"Over here," she whispered to Nikki

"Let's go a little further, this is kind of embarrassing."

They walked deeper into the woods.

"Can I ask you something?" Nikki asked with hesitation.

"Sure."

"Well, you don't seem very scared."

Veronica paused. Nikki stopped and looked at her. She wanted to know how Veronica did it. How she seemed so cool under pressure. What Nikki really wanted was to tell someone that she was frightened out of her mind. She was too embarrassed to mention her fear to the men. She just kept quiet around the boys and listened; it was all she could do to keep from shutting down. She could pretend while they were around but out here in the quiet woods, she suddenly felt like talking.

"Nik, I am scared," Veronica said to Nikki with eyes that flashed a terrible honesty. "I am terrified that I do not know what is going on," she said vulnerable now for the first time.

"But you're dealing with everything so well, like the boys are. You blinded that lady with the paint thing while I just stood there. I couldn't move. It was like it was happening to someone else and I was just watching." Nikki began to breathe deeper with the release of her fears. Veronica put her arms around the frightened girl.

"You were in shock, it is to be expected. People respond to extreme situations differently." She held Nikki for a moment and heard her sniffle. Veronica worried that the young woman might start to lose her mind. She had to help the poor girl. Her human compassion needed her to help Nikki.

"The more you experience stressful situations, the easier it is to keep your head in the moment," Veronica said letting her go. Nikki had a tear in her eye but she was listening. *Good*, Veronica thought, *I am getting through to her.*

"I have seen some rather horrible things. You just have to take a deep breath and tell yourself; this is happening, I have to deal with it."

"What are you talking about, horrible things, how could anything be more horrible than today?" Nikki said frustrated.

"Did you ever hear about the earthquake in San Francisco back in 1989?"

"Yeah, the bridge collapsed, I saw it on T.V."

"A lot of things collapsed," Veronica said with sadness. She leaned up against a tree, her body suddenly feeling very heavy. Nikki looked at her noticing how she had seemed to change. The tall strong Veronica, who had snapped into action to help the bitten woman, then later had the forethought to blind the thing with a paint gun, now seemed vulnerable. She appeared hesitant, as if she were confessing some long hidden secret. Nikki decided to give her some privacy. The pressure in her bladder was enormous. She found a small bush, still within earshot and prepared to pee. Veronica appreciated the moment. She looked out over the woods away from Nikki and continued.

"My dad and I were on our way to a baseball game; the World Series," Veronica suppressed a laugh. "The ground shook violently. We found ourselves near a collapsed freeway. My dad was a surgeon so we parked. My dad wanted to go into the smashed rubble and put himself at risk. He wanted to leave me in the car while he pulled people out. I begged him not to go."

Nikki, enthralled by the story, finished and buttoned up her pants. She had an uncomfortable urge to flush something. She kicked a few leaves over the puddle and walked back to Veronica.

"I could tell that he really wanted to go in. He wanted to crawl around the burning wrecks and save as many people as he could. That was the kind of a man he was. But I begged him not to. He was all I had. My mother died when I was born. I did not want him to leave me too. What if there was an aftershock? He would have been trapped in there."

Nikki looked at her with the understanding of a dear friend.

"What happened?" she asked in a whisper.

"He decided not to go in even though I know he wanted to. He stayed with me. Many people showed up, firemen, some police, and a number of civilians; just normal people who wanted to help. They started to bring the injured to us. My dad always carried a medical bag; a field kit, he called it. So we cleared out an area inside a carpet store and set up a triage."

Veronica leaned up off the tree. She sat on the cool earth and continued.

"I was eleven years old, surrounded by bleeding patients. I knew most of my dad's instruments. I assisted him. He asked for something, and I handed it to him. We clamped arteries with hemostats, cleaned lacerations with saline, packed gauze in open wounds, and prepared patients for the ambulances. It was a hell of a thing for an eleven year old to see."

"My God, how did you deal with that?" Nikki asked quietly. Veronica looked up at her with resolve. As she stood, she appeared to revert back into her composed persona.

"You set priorities, my dad would say. You figure out to the best of your abilities what needs to be done and you do it." She put her hand on Nikki's shoulder gently. "Right now we need to get out of here and let the police know what happened. If anything gets in our way, we deal with it. We just have to remain as calm as possible and keep our heads."

Nikki looked very frightened. Veronica put her arms around the small young woman and remembered something her father said to her after the quake and the chaos.

"After it was over, my dad said that I had been through something that would change me forever. Everything was different after the quake. I was different. He said that surviving the experience would make me stronger," Veronica said in a trembling voice, holding back her tears as she spoke her father's words. She squeezed Nikki tight while missing her late father.

Nikki nodded, feeling strengthened. Veronica let her go and began to walk towards a bush of her own. She did not want to look Nikki in the eye, her emotions needed to settle first.

"What do you think of the boys?" Nikki asked.

Veronica stopped and thought.

"I think they are fine. We will be okay with them." *Dad would have liked Jack*, she thought.

"What do we have?" Mason asked while looking at an array of items that Tony had laid out on the workbench.

"Nine modified .410 shot shells for a breach loading squirrel gun, eleven rounds of .380 for my pistol, two half full paint guns, screwdrivers, two hammers, a machete, a pick axe, two shovels, a wood axe and our knives," he listed in rapid succession. Mason picked up his paint gun and removed the barrel.

"Remember the blow guns we used to make?" he asked.

Tony retrieved a roll of duct tape from the handlebars of his bike.

They worked fast. The men were experienced in making blow darts from their youth. Jack had come up with the idea when they were fifteen after watching a documentary about the Cherokee tribe using river reeds to make blow pipes. His approach was to use a quarter inch copper tube in place of reeds. The darts were fashioned from bamboo skewers used in cooking. Jack had devised a paper cone attached to the skewers, covered with tape that was cut to match the diameter of the pipe. After a little practice, the two hooligans were trying out all sorts of materials for blow darts. Nails, with paper cones, skewers of different length, sometimes counter balanced with a small ring of tape at the front, even tiny arrow heads on the skewers made from scalpel blades. Blow darts adorned almost every telephone pole in the neighborhood that year and for years to come.

Mason picked out six of the largest nails that he could find in the metal container. Tony found a Penthouse magazine from September 1984 in one of the crates. They used the centerfold to make the paper cones and affixed them to the backs of the nails with tape. They then placed the darts into the end of a paint gun barrel. Using a small pair of scissors from Tony's first aid kit, they trimmed the ends down to the proper size. Soon they had six sharp projectiles. Jack checked his watch. It read five thirty.

"It's getting late. I wonder if we should stay here tonight and get started at first light," Jack said.

Tony was looking at the Penthouse magazine, perusing the dirty pictures.

"I don't want to stay here longer than we have to."

"If you run out of gas at seven and the sun goes down about eight thirty, we have no way of knowing how long we'd be walking in the dark," Mason said.

Tony saw his point. He turned the page of the naughty magazine examining the images. Jack studied his friend. He appeared to be handling things alright despite what they had been through. Before Jack could inquire about his friend's state of mind, Tony spoke.

"How are you doing with all this shit?" Tony asked without looking up from his magazine.

"Fine, considering, I'll feel better when we get these chicks back to town," Jack answered. "What about you?"

"I never shot anyone until today. It was weird. The gun put a kooky distance between me and, well, killing. It was too simple to just pull the trigger. I mean I know what I did and that I had to do it. I guess the training took over," Tony answered. He found himself thankful for all the practice that he and Jack had participated in while growing up. He felt a little strange but he wanted to say something to his brother.

"You know, I just wanted to say, incase we don't make it…"

Jack cut him off.

"No, don't. I know what you mean but we are going to get out of this." Jack said with reassurance. He loved Tony like a brother yet thought it best to stay away from any talk of finality. It was important that they both keep their mental edge for whatever came next. Thoughts of their possible demise were counter productive and could fuel self doubt. Tony did not hesitate to shoot when he needed to, that was good. He had to keep his brother's mind focused on the positive.

"Tony, we know what we are doing. We are armed and ready. If we have to walk over the top of this mountain, we'll be fine. I'll kill a deer for the girls and we can camp our way back to the world. We can handle it. We have been getting away with crazy shit for fifteen years," Mason said with resolve.

Tony knew he was right. He was glad that Mason was with him. Throughout their youth the two friends had always escaped serious trouble. He felt that Jack was his good luck charm.

"We always get away with it," said Tony.

"Yeah, we sort of do" he answered smiling.

Thirty

Upon seeing the shack from the road, Lance dropped down into a crouching run. He thought that there may be something in the structure that he could use, perhaps something to drink. Walking in the hot sun had given him a tremendous thirst. As he moved closer he heard voices. He slowed his footsteps to move quieter while reaching his left hand towards the door.

Entering the clearing from the trees, Veronica was the first to see a man with a shotgun enter the door to the shack. She froze expecting to hear a blast kill her new friends.

"Oh shit!" Nikki cursed under her breath. Veronica pulled the pistol from her pocket. She looked at it for a moment and found the safety. The weapon that her father had taught her to shoot with was different than Tony's gun. She switched the gun to fire and moved carefully towards the shack.

"Wait here," she whispered with her hand back in a stop gesture. Nikki looked around the empty forest for a moment. *Screw that*, she thought and followed behind Veronica, trying to stay quiet.

Lance burst through the door and caught the men unaware. Tony dropped the Penthouse magazine. It fell open on the floor; a black and white picture of a dethroned Miss America stared up with a wanton look. Both men froze, held at bay by a twelve gauge shotgun.

"What's this, a circle jerk?" Lance quipped.

Mason scanned a mental inventory of choices. He put his hands up and slowly side stepped to his right under the pretense of adjusting his posture. The further he could get from Tony, the better chance one of them would have to survive. He knew that a twelve gauge shot a wide pattern at its target but that pattern dissipated over distance. If he could get far enough away from Tony, a single blast from the shotgun would only hit one of them, not both. It was a long shot but it was something.

"What are you doing here Hoss?" Lance asked, still in the doorway.

Mason gestured with his right hand towards the motorcycles, moving yet another step away from Tony with the movement.

"My bike overheats. Had to stop for a while," Mason lied.

"Which one?" Lance demanded, casting a greedy eye at the bikes.

"The Kawasaki, I got a bad cylinder."

Tony looked at Mason, understanding his plan. If the guy was going to steal a bike, give him the one with the poor gas mileage. He saw Mason nudge his foot to the right and wondered why.

"Well, what say I borrow it for a spell?" Lance smiled. Suddenly, he felt the barrel of a pistol against his head, pushing hard just behind his right ear.

"What say you put your gun down, slowly," Veronica said holding Tony's gun. Lance froze but he was not about to give in just yet.

"Hey, your not going to shoot me now, are ya darling?"

Veronica cocked the hammer of the pistol back. The sound of the weapon resounded loudly in Lance's ear.

"I am going to spray your cerebellum all over this door if you do not put that gun down now!" she said in a near growl.

Lance believed her. He suddenly felt very queasy. He stretched the rifle out far from his body with his arms wide. Mason approached quickly, grasped the rifle and brought his fist up underneath Lance's chin, cracking one of his perfect incisors. Lance lost consciousness with a bright flash of light from behind his eyes.

"I am going to spray your cerebellum all over the door?" Jack teased towards Veronica with a disbelieving smile. He and Tony were using duct tape to secure Lance's arms and legs. Veronica blushed slightly at the friendly taunts.

"Cerebellum?" Jack smiled.

"I like to be specific," she said in her defense, brushing her now troublesome hair out of her face once again. The men sat Lance's limp body in a corner near the bench. Mason stood and checked the shotgun, cycling out a shell and reinserting it, then switching the gun to safe.

"Check his pockets," he said.

Tony was already doing just that. He produced three twelve gauge rounds and a twenty dollar bill.

"Any one need toilet paper," he said holding up the cash. Nikki giggled, finding the comment strangely funny. She was glad to see Lance tied up. *That spoiled asshole ran around town for years like he was at the top of the food chain.* It pleased her to see him humbled. Then a thought occurred to her.

"How did he get out here?" Nikki asked realizing the importance of the question. *If he had a vehicle, we wouldn't have to walk. Why then would he have wanted to steal one of the motorcycles?* Her hopes dashed at the thought.

"Good question," Tony said. He slapped his prisoner across the face. "Wake up shit kicker."

Lance roused struggling against his bonds. He moved about as if he were tangled up in blankets. As his awareness increased, he thrashed about startled. Opening his eyes he saw Mason standing over him, grinning.

"Morning sunshine."

Memory returned and Lance relaxed into submission. He was in trouble. He would have to play along and try to get out of the situation.

"Hey," he acknowledged while avoiding Mason's gaze. His hands were firmly secured behind his back. As he edged himself up against the wall, he slipped uncomfortably down on his neck. Tony, on one knee, grabbed him by the shoulders and helped him back to a leaning position. He stood leaving Lance to consider his fate.

"Hey," Mason said low, a devious look in his eye. "You were going to steal a bike and take off, weren't you?"

"N-no, I just wanted a ride, a ride away from those things," Lance said in a trembling voice.

"What happened to your truck?" Veronica asked.

"Josh and Zeke were bit; they went crazy a mile back. We went off the road and broke an axle. They're dead." Lance averted his eyes as if the loss of his friends mattered to him.

"How far is the truck?" Tony asked for confirmation.

"About a mile, but its busted. Do you have some water?" Lance whined.

Veronica stooped to give Lance the last of her bottled water. She tipped the bottle up for him. He drank in loud gulps without spilling. Tony approached Mason and spoke in hushed tones.

"Can we drain his gas and mix it with what I have left?"

"No, it'll still be too rich, we don't have any oil" Mason said.

Nikki, finding her senses sharpened in their current dilemma, overheard the conversation. The idea of having to walk through the forest still frightened her. She spoke.

"Why do you need oil?" her young voice asked.

"Bikes don't use straight gas, you have to mix it with a special kind of oil," Tony said turning his attention to her. She was standing in the far corner of the shack, nearest the door with her arms crossed. Tony moved near her.

"How are you holding up?" he asked in his kind manner.

"Oh you know, I wish I was home," she shrugged her delicate shoulders with a reluctant smile.

"How far is it back to town?" Mason asked Lance.

"About four more hours of driving, I don't know how many miles."

Mason sat on the milk crate near Lance with a frown. Tony had seen the look before. Mason was thinking; thinking hard about something that he might not want to get into. It was the face that Jack made when he had an idea that might not work. The face he wore when he was about to put all of his chips in at the poker table. Tony thought that Jack was in that moment where he was deciding whether or not to mention his idea. Mason drummed his fingers on the milk crate underneath him. He looked at the crate between his legs and his expression changed. He had decided that his idea was valid.

"Do you have jumper cables in your truck?" Mason inquired to Lance.

"Yeah, behind the seat."

"Is your battery good?"

Lance's expression went blank. He did not understand the line of questions. Tony took one step forward; he saw where Mason was heading. It could be a good idea or it could get them killed.

"Yeah, brand new last month, why?" Lance asked realizing with his tongue that the throbbing in his upper lip was a chipped tooth.

Mason stood and looked at Tony who had a severe look on his face.

"Dude…" Tony said.

"It gets us all out of here, but we would have to wait until morning." Mason offered to Tony. Veronica moved next to Mason and without realizing it, put a hand on his forearm.

"What gets us out of here?" she asked.

Thirty One

Nikki sat on the brown grass of the clearing watching Tony dig a small fire pit. Her thoughts were a cloud of disappointment. On one hand she did not like the idea of sleeping out in the woods. On the other, she did not relish the alternative of walking for hours in the dark. Jack said they could make torches to light their way but that brought her little comfort. She was not lazy. She would walk under normal circumstances. Exercise was enjoyable to Nikki and she was in fine shape, but the thought of creeping through the dark unknown made her legs weak. Jack had a plan that he said he would explain over dinner. So now, as the sun fell behind the high hills, she watched the boys make a fire.

Mason arrived with some heavy rocks. He lined the pit with the stones and proceeded to locate more. Nikki rose to her feet to help. She felt out of place. Everyone knew what to do except her. Nikki decided to follow Jack and copy his actions. She found some smaller rocks and brought them to the pit, her white paintball shirt became soiled in the effort.

"Thanks," Jack said to her when she dropped the rocks for him to sort around the ring. Veronica brought an arm full of dried wood that she had scavenged from the area. Nikki decided to look for wood as well, albeit not very far from the shack. As the sky dropped from bright orange to dark grey, they gathered in front of the fire.

Tony was very helpful to Nikki as he walked her through the finer points of dining in the woods. She had chosen a can of spaghetti and meatballs. Tony opened the can with the can opener on his Leatherman tool, leaving the lid partially on, bent back as a handle. He did the same for two cans of chili and placed them all on the perimeter of the fire to cook. Mason had carved two medium sized spoon-like objects from dried birch branches for the women as eating utensils. He ran them over the fire a few times on the end of his combat knife to seal them from moisture. A few carvings later, he and Tony had two functional sets of chop sticks, sealed in the same manner. Nikki watched the boys work, fascinated by their comfort and proficiency in the great outdoors. Camping was not her kind of activity.

Jack and Veronica ate chili; Tony dined on two small uncooked cans of salmon. They ate in silence, holding the hot cans in thick motorcycle gloves. The women enjoyed two of the lukewarm Cokes, while the men drank from their canteens. After the meal, with darkness setting in, Jack began to speak.

"Okay, I have been thinking about it and I think we have a good plan." All eyes were on Jack as he continued. "Tony and I head to Dickhead's truck, swipe his battery and jumper cables, then back into camp and get my truck." Nikki tensed at the thought of the men returning to camp.

"What if you can't get to it? What if those things are around?" Nikki pleaded. Veronica looked hard into the fire as if there was some question to be answered within the flames.

"Well, I was thinking that we might get back and find the place full of cops. We can get help then. If not, if those things are still there, we coast in as quietly as possible, get the truck and get out. I have a full tank of gas; it will get us up and over this mountain; back to town." He looked at Veronica

"Unless you want to ride out tomorrow and take our chances walking," Jack said to her. She looked at him concerned, the firelight making her sharp features very beautiful.

"Four hours drive in a truck, what is that, approximately fifty miles?" Veronica asked.

"Depends, but that's the thing, we don't know. This is just about all of our food. That's not a problem, but water?" he said leaning away from the flames. Tony stood stretching.

"With these hills over a great distance," Tony said doubtful, "in the sun with no water. A four hour drive could turn into a two day hike."

"Dehydration," Veronica said.

Nikki cringed. She did not want the men to go back to the camp, leaving her and Veronica. She feared what would happen if they did not make it back. Tony walked away, disappearing into the shack. She watched Veronica.

"Does that mean he agrees?" Veronica asked turning to look at Jack.

"Yeah, he knows what's up," Jack answered weary.

"You will be careful?" Veronica urged quietly.

"Yep," he said self assured. They looked at each other for a long moment, Veronica breaking away first to stare at the fire. Nikki wondered if they were interested in each other. Silence sat in the air. Tony returned with four chocolate health bars.

"Dessert, anyone?" he asked handing a bar to Nikki. Veronica looked up, deep in thought and declined the offer with a wave. Suddenly she had no appetite. Jack accepted.

"Do you want to take the first watch?" Jack asked Tony.

"No, you do it, I'll feel better if you're well rested before we ride out," Tony answered. He wanted Jack's senses sharp for their morning ride into hell. Jack was right; getting the truck was the only way to get out of the hills. Tony thought he and Jack might be able to make it but the girls could have a hard time in the heat. They could not gamble on finding water on the way. Water flows downhill, so the higher you go in the mountains, the less you are likely to find. There were four bottles of water and two cokes left by his count, not enough at all for a trek into the unknown.

Tony rose again to his feet to check on their prisoner. Walking into the shack he saw Lance in the shadows. Tony had taped his hands in front of his body so that Lance could eat three health bars. He gave Lance a beer rather than give him any of their dwindling water supplies. Tony did not know why he was even bothering to help the man who had held he and Jack at gunpoint hours earlier. He felt a touch of human compassion and fed Lance because it is how he would like to be treated. Prisoners, even asshole prisoners were still human beings.

"You all right?" he asked checking the tape on Lance's wrists.

"Yeah," the bound man grumbled. Lance was hungry. The bars were not enough but he was not about to ask for anything. The duct tape was uncomfortable and he was tired. After Tony left the structure to return to his friends, Lance thought he would try to rest.

If he could sleep for a while he might wake up while the rest of them were asleep. That would give him time to work on his restraints. He could probably chew the tape free if he had some time alone. Lance pushed himself forward, sliding on the floor to a fetal position with his back to the door. He curled up wondering how he had gotten into this mess. He thought to himself that he should have just fired his gun when he opened the door. He should have taken out both men and rode off. Lying on the stiff plywood floor he opened his eyes for a moment. Flickering firelight seeped in through the small spaces between the planks of the wall. Something from underneath the workbench shined with a pale gold shimmer. Lance reached out and found a single .410 shotgun shell. He grasped it quickly and slid the round into his pocket. Looking over his shoulder to be sure he was alone, he made a chipped tooth grin. If he could get his hands free and get a weapon, this time he would not hesitate.

Tony returned to the fire to see Jack rise to his feet.

"I am gonna go that way about fifty yards," Jack said indicating with a nod, "Come get me around two."

"Do you think any of those things followed us?" Tony asked.

"Not really but I would rather keep a look out," Jack said and trudged off holding the twelve gauge. Veronica watched him depart, taking note of his direction. Tony sat next to Nikki.

"Do you think those people will try to get us?" Nikki asked in a low tone.

He shook his head to reassure her, though he was not sure. He thought he would try to get her mind off of things. Tony pulled out his pistol.

"Have you ever fired a gun?" he asked, removing the magazine. He moved back the slide and dropped the chambered round into his hand.

"No, never even held one," she said with interest. The weapon was small and light, not the kind of gun she would expect a man like Tony to have.

"Why is it so small?" she asked feeling the balance of the weapon.

"It's not the size of the gun, it's how good you can shoot", he answered. Veronica snorted, holding back a laugh at his blatant innuendo. She rose, tired, to her feet.

"I am going to try and get some rest." She said looking out into the dark night. "Don't stay up too late you two."

"'Night," Nikki said holding the pistol.

Tony spent an hour showing the young woman how the weapon worked. From the composition of a bullet, the explosive gasses released in the powder and the copper covered projectile, to the mechanics of how one bullet is ejected and replaced by another. He had her remove and replace the magazine, as well as showed her how to reload and move a fresh round into the chamber. The determined young lady practiced over and over loading the gun, switching the safety off and taking aim. Nikki was a good student and paid close attention. He showed her all that he could short of firing the weapon. After the fire had died down, around ten, they went into the shack. Tony made her a small pillow by stuffing his extra gauze bandages into a small utility pack from his harness. He curled up in the corner next to the door, Nikki slept across the room in the other. He watched her with care until she fell asleep.

Thirty Two

The warm blue grey shades of the forest night were both comforting and foreboding. The moderate temperature and lack of illumination would be relaxing to Jack Mason, if the situation were not so dire. The moonless night made his eyes prone to slumber. His muscles were starting to fatigue after the events of so long a day. The fighting, the interspersed blasts of adrenalin, and even maintaining control of his motorcycle had taken its toll. As he replayed his memories in his mind, he wondered if it was all just a bad dream. *No,* he thought to himself, *believe it or not, this shit is real.* He had to keep sharp and keep a look out. People were counting on him.

Mason rubbed his eyes and focused on the road ahead. He had found himself a small gully next to the road about seventy yards away from the shack. There were plenty of bushes and small trees behind him for cover and the naturally formed earth concealed his position from the front. He had chosen to lay prone and keep his view on the road where he assumed the creatures would approach from. That is if they came this way. He had no idea what those things were or what they would do. He was afraid that they could smell uninfected people. The blinded woman seemed to sniff at the air towards Tony. If they could smell people, then they might be on their way. That was a long shot, but just incase, Mason would be there to protect his friends.

Lying prone was not the best way for Mason to stay awake. He had to shake off the cobwebs off his mind. The road before him was barely perceivable in the starlight. Mason was blessed with good eyes as well as experience with hunting in the forest, but in his tired state, the image of the road was becoming less real to his perception. It seemed as if he were looking at a black and white photograph. He was thankful for a small breeze that would move the foliage from time to time adding movement to the scene, reassuring Mason that he was awake. Then a noise from behind his position sent a sickening shot glass of pure adrenalin to his gut.

Mason silently rolled to his left side, keeping the shotgun extended in line with is right leg. He leaned up on his left arm and raised his head to listen. His right ear became his main sensory organ as he calmed himself to become more attentive. The slight breeze dissipated and in the distance he heard small footsteps. The slight crunching of dry grass told Mason that the person who was approaching was ether very careful about being quiet or they were not very heavy. Mason decided to discreetly inquire who it was. He made a double clicking noise with is mouth; the kind of click that John Wayne would make in the movies to get his horse to move.

"Click, click."

The footfalls stopped suddenly.

"Psst," sounded in the night. It was Veronica approaching. Mason was surprised that she was able to come so close before he had noticed. Her attractive form crouched down as she crept towards Jack unsure of just where he was in the darkness.

"Where are you?" she whispered.

"Five steps forward then down a yard on your right," he answered as quiet as he could manage with his deep voice. His throat crackled slightly when he spoke and he realized that he was thirsty. Veronica took to her knees and offered Jack a Coke.

"I thought you could use some caffeine." She handed him the can. He took it and slid it underneath his shirt. He opened the can slowly to hide the sound beneath the cloth as best as he could. Veronica noticed this and laid herself out in the gully next to Jack, not seductively but rather to hide her silhouette.

"Are you always so careful?" she asked.

"No need to call extra attention to ourselves," he whispered.

He turned to look down the road once again. Veronica rolled a quarter turn to become prone herself, stomach down flat on the earth and scanned the area as well.

"Do you want me to leave?" she offered continuing to whisper.

"No, I can use the company," he said sipping a large drink of the soda. A shooting star blazed across the heavens causing them both to look up.

"Seen a few of those tonight," he said.

They were quiet. Veronica rolled on her back to look into the sky. Small flecks of light were visible above the rolling clouds. Little bits of floating fluff were flowing in the air back down the road, towards camp. They looked amazing in the quiet night.

"So, what's your story, are you a nurse or something?" Jack asked while keeping watch.

"No, actually I am a premed student. Why?"

"Cerebellum," he joked. She blushed, though Jack could see it.

"Yes, I like to be specific." She put her hands peacefully on her stomach while watching the sky. Another shooting star flew by. The clouds seemed to stop moving, frozen in the stratosphere.

"I love medicine and science. How the body works and how to cure people has always interested me. I just wish I knew what was going on out there. I wish I had a sample of their blood to analyze so I could learn what is behind this," she said frustrated.

"I guess I could get you some of their blood."

"No, that might be dangerous," she said turning her head to Jack. "Since we are dealing with a possible pathogen, exposure to their blood may prove to be infectious." She reached out and touched his elbow. "You cannot let their blood get on you, in your eyes or mouth or a cut; there is a chance it could make you sick."

He looked in her direction even though he could not see her face in the dark. He wondered what she looked like right now. What would her expression tell him?

"Okay, we will be careful. Tony can take the twelve gauge and I'll use my sword. I want you guys to have Tony's pistol and the .410 until we get back, just in case."

"You have to be careful with the sword. In medicine we call it sharps precautions. You have to make sure that you do not cut yourself after it has been exposed to contaminants," she said removing her hand from his arm.

"Sharps precautions, got it. What else do you have? Any theories?" he asked.

Veronica breathed deep, thinking. She needed a lab, a spectroscope, an MRI, and a specimen to examine. She needed to finish med school to be able to even start asking the right questions. She considered the events of the day with her keen memory.

"Well, I cannot be sure about anything, these are just observations and assumptions," she said unsure. "I think that they breathe, the growling is evidence of that however, I am not sure they have a heartbeat. The ones at the camp had very little blood pressure when they were shot," she paused to consider further.

Jack was impressed. She was sharp and appeared to be thinking things through very clearly. He thought of the blinded woman.

"What about smell?" he asked.

"Yes, I did notice a slight chemical odor, not unlike ammonia," she answered.

"No, I mean yes, I noticed that too but I meant their sense of smell."

"The woman at camp seemed to detect your friend by his scent. That is frightening," Veronica said closing her eyes. "Do you think they could do it over great distances?"

"Animals can," he said while looking down the road again. Feeling a breeze on his face he noticed that the wind had changed. *Good*, Jack thought, *stay downwind of the bastards.*

"What do you think the weird smell that they have is about?" Jack asked.

"I really do not know. Some sort of chemical process in their blood, perhaps it is from the infection itself. You would have to ask someone a lot smarter than me," she said exhausted.

"What time is it?" she asked.

Jack closed his right eye and hit the light on his G-Shock watch for a split second. The brightness burned an image into his left retina that read 11:30. The image would stay in his left eye for several seconds until his pupil dilated back to full aperture. By keeping his right eye closed, he was able to protect some of his night vision.

"Eleven thirty."

Veronica forced herself to relax. Twelve hours ago she was worried about opening up to a man and now everything had changed. Her world had changed once again due to some tragedy that she could not control. Somehow she would make it. The men would return and they would get out. If not, she would drag Nikki up the mountain by herself if she had to. Jack and Tony would be alright and she would go on with her life like she had planned. Learn to trust, learn to love, and learn how to live.

"If we get out of this," she said without really realizing that she was speaking, "I would like to make you dinner." There it was out. In a way it frightened her that she actually said the words. Her question was not too forward, but absolutely unprecedented for Veronica. She kept her eyes shut and waited.

"I would like that," Jack's deep voice whispered.

Veronica breathed in a deep breath, feeling relaxation fall over her. She smiled. Moments later she heard Tony's voice talking to Jack.

"No, nothing at all," Jack said. She opened her eyes and saw Jack standing. He offered her his hand and she took it. Rising to her feet with his help she understood that she had fallen asleep. It was time for Tony to take over the watch. She walked with drowsy steps towards the shack. Looking up she saw the clouds racing away now from the campground and all their troubles. The winds had changed. Inside, she soon fell back into to a dreamless sleep.

A few miles away in the quiet camp of Professor Galloway, several once living students milled about without direction. They had all partaken of poor Ranger Watkins and subsequently, without prey, staggered their stiff forms around the camp without reason. They did not tire so they did not require sleep. The darkness did not frighten them for they had no fear. Their only purpose, only motivation, would be more living matter to consume. At around three A.M. in the pitch black, it arrived. Born on the changing wind came something to strive for; a faint scent of something desirable, something warm and wet, to devour. One by one they moved slowly towards the smell. Falling and stumbling in the dark, they came slowly but undaunted.

Thirty Three

Mason stood next to the workbench holding up the barrel of his paint gun. Nikki and Veronica watched his demonstration as soft morning light illuminated the shack. He placed a nail dart in the barrel, pushed the end down with his thumb and blew a large blast of air from his mouth through the pipe. A four inch nail stuck solidly into a pine two by four in the wall. Nikki raised her eyebrows in surprise.

"See, now the principal is the same for the paint guns, but with a lot more pressure," he said retrieving the dart, careful not to crush the paper and tape cone. He placed the dart in the tube again and screwed the barrel back on to the paint gun.

"You have to load the darts one at a time and you'll have to be close to get through bone. This is a last resort, but it's an option I want you to know about," he said.

Mason looked around the shack. The motorcycles were checked out and parked outside. Tony had taken Lance to pee so he could not beg the girls later to take him out and attempt an escape. Mason had affixed a two by four across the door that should hold well. He did not expect a siege but he was worried about leaving the girls alone. Even though he had known them for only a day, he cared about them. He looked at Veronica and toyed with the idea of going alone, leaving Tony to watch out for the women. This was a two man job, if something happened to one of them on the way; the other had to complete the mission.

"Here they come," Nikki said looking outside. Tony emerged through the door with Lance in his charge. Setting him back in the corner, Tony checked his restraints. Standing, he looked to Mason. It was time to go. Mason approached Lance while Tony walked outside to his bike followed by Nikki.

"Check it out man," Mason said with all seriousness, "We are going to go get my truck and then we are all going to get out of here, even you. If you give these girls any shit, I will drive you back to the campground, cover your ass in barbeque sauce and dump you in front of those things."

Lance cowered at the thought and nodded his reluctant acknowledgement.

Outside, Nikki assisted Tony as he adjusted his equipment. He was clad in his motorcycle boots and plastic armor. Nikki held his combat harness so that he could slide into it like a coat. He strapped down his gear firmly and felt the fit. The twelve gauge shotgun was taped to his handlebars. Removing his combat knife he sliced off the trigger finger of his right glove.

"What did you do that for?" Nikki asked looking at his glove.

"The fabric gets in the way of the trigger" he said wiggling his naked finger in a trigger pulling motion.

Mason pulled on his gear in a similar fashion. He had his scabbard duct tapped to his handlebars and one of the milk crates secured with rope and tape to his back fender. Veronica stood next to him holding the .410 as he mounted his bike.

"Sure you don't want to take this?" Veronica asked indicating the shotgun. Mason shook his head.

"No, if we don't make it back it's up to you to get her out of here. Leave asshole dude here if it comes to that. If he gets out of hand," Mason put a finger in the shape of a gun to his head, "Cerebellum."

"Count on it," she said lifting the weapon.

Inside the shack, Lance knew he did not have much time. He had managed to lift his arms high enough to grasp one of the homemade darts off the workbench. Holding it in both hands he tried to poke the sharp end into the tape around his wrists but lacked the flexibility to do so. In a panic, he dropped the dart on the floor and hid it with his leg. He brought his wrists to his mouth and tried to chew the tape. All he succeeded to do was wet the tape and crush its fibers. Frustrated and afraid, he gnawed harder, but to no avail. Pain flashed from his teeth up through the nerves of his face. The tape snagged on the rough surface of his broken tooth. The sensation was electric agony. He looked at the tape and saw that it had frayed. He endured tremendous pain as he slowly worked his bonds over the jagged surface of his broken tooth.

"Be careful," Nikki said to Tony, "seriously."

"Don't worry; we'll be back in no time." He pulled out his pistol and spare magazine, "Here, keep this for me."

She took the weapon, checked the safety like he had shown her and put it in her pocket. Mason, helmet on and ready to go, kicked over his starter. Nikki handed Tony his helmet. Her concern was apparent. She was afraid for the boys; afraid she would not see them again. Veronica put her arm around Nikki as she backed away from the bikes. Tony kicked his starter three times and his old yellow bike sputtered to life. *Come on girl*, he thought, *you got a lot left in you*. Nikki looked at the rear fender of Tony's Yamaha and noticed a worn sticker that said *Suck Ass*. She smiled despite her worry.

The two bikes, unencumbered by extra passengers, blasted onto the road. Mason, in the lead, popped his front wheel in the air and disappeared over the rise.

Lance had almost snagged his way through the tape when he heard the women approach. Pain induced sweat covered his face. He quickly tried to brush off the sweat. He put his hands down, hoping that no one would notice the frayed tape on his wrists. As they entered, he pretended to be sleeping.

"How long do we wait?" Nikki asked removing the pistol from her pocket and holding it for comfort.

"Jack said two and a half hours," she answered checking the watch that he had given her. The watch read seven A.M. Veronica placed the two by four across the door.

The sunrise had allowed the ghouls see once again. The tempting scent had faded with the dawn but they were close. They moved faster now and no longer stumbled. The noise that roared in the distance gave them a new heading. It was a loud sound that echoed in their dead ears calling for investigation. Once young bodies, healthy and strong now moved their torn and mangled carcasses, mouth first towards the sound of motorcycles.

Thirty Four

The ruts and rivulets of the hard dirt road seemed easier to navigate at higher speeds. Tony strived to match Mason's pace but his best friend was the better rider. This was urgent work and he knew how Mason would push himself to get the job done. Tony hoped that he would be able to keep up, and most important, not let his friend down. Rounding the second turn in the road, Mason slowed and trained his eyes off to the side. Lance had given him an approximate location for his broken down truck. Providing that he was telling the truth, this should be the place. Mason dropped his bike into first gear. Putting along in jerky spurts, he scanned the hillside beneath him. He saw it, about one hundred yards away down the hill. Looking back he observed that Tony saw it too. Mason cranked his throttle and bucked his cycle over the rise. He switched to second gear while keeping a careful eye out for surprise geography that might fell his bike. The ground was safe with the exception of the large gully that had trapped the Dodge. Mason saw a lip on the top of the gully that could serve as a springboard for his cycle. He hit the edge and jumped four feet, landing on the other side. Riding a perimeter around the vehicle, he made sure that the coast was clear. Seeing the slumped pile of human remains in the dirt, he squeezed his clutch lever and slowed to a halt. A cloud of flies, disturbed by his arrival, flew up into the air angry at Mason's intrusion. He was not sure if it was his imagination but he thought he could hear their buzzing over his motor. Mason saw the body but tried to be distant, scientific, like Veronica would be. He took note of its decaying wounds but tried to not let the reality of it in. He killed the engine and leaned his bike on the truck.

Tony was not the motorcycle enthusiast that Mason was. He decelerated before hitting the gully and left his bike to idle on the kickstand. He jumped the gully, just not on his motorcycle. He landed on the dry grass with an awkward thump. Opening the driver's door, his senses were assaulted by the decaying fermentation of Josh's body. The smell pushed Tony back as if it were a physical force. He swung out, away from the baking cloud and hung from the door by his hand. He made an audible groan. Mason heard and lifted his head over the truck bed to check on his friend.

"What's up?" he inquired.

"Open the door, air it out!" Tony declared, sure that he would never forget the sour smell.

The flies settled back to their work of eating and laying eggs in the rotting corpse. Mason walked carefully around, not wishing to disturb their toil for some strange reason, and opened the passenger's door. A light breeze blew through the cab sending the stink of rotting flesh in Mason's face. His squinted down hard at the wretched air.

Inside the cab, he saw the work that Lance's twelve gauge had done. The tissue around the exposed meat that once made up the seated man had curled back on itself forming bizarre skin blossoms. His midsection had bloated and filled with gas. The disgusting juicy bits that should be dark red or even brown from exposure to heat and air had turned a greenish black. Mason noticed this distinction by way of comparison to the exposed muscle of the corpse on the ground. One was in the heat of the truck all day, and the other was not, but there was another difference. The sad fly covered scoop of human remains lacked the same smell. It smelled like rotting meat, without the tinge of ammonia. He would remember what he had seen for Veronica. She would want to know all about his observations.

Tony took a deep breath, held it, and shot his arm into the cab to find the hood release lever. He pulled the lever and quickly threw the drivers seat forward to look for the jumper cables. He scrambled his right hand around in a hectic search. He felt the cables and pulled them free. Kicking the door closed, he fell on the ground.

"That... is...fucking... disgusting," he gasped.

Mason walked to the front of the truck and opened the hood. Much to his relief, he saw that the battery was undamaged. He pulled a wrench from the cargo pocket of his camouflage pants and started to remove the battery. Tony got to his feet, coiled up the loose strands of jumper cable while walking to Mason's bike and put the cable in the milk crate. He saw the flies. He saw the body, so pathetic and forlorn, piled in an impossibly uncomfortable position. The man's arms were splayed out in opposite directions that must have dislocated something somewhere. Tony quickly turned and pulled off his helmet. He thought he was going to throw up his very soul. He leaned on the back of the truck breathing heavily. The image of the body sat in his thoughts. It was so sad and distorted; it hardly looked like it was once a person; a person with hopes and dreams. The finality of the man's death, the indignity of his last resting place brought hot tears to Tony's eyes. He knew that he could not fall apart now. Things had to be done. He thought about the girls at the shack and about Jack who needed his help. He remembered his

Shakespeare and tales of proud deeds. He had to steel his heart for just a little bit longer.

Mason moved from the front of the truck to his bike. He placed the battery in the milk crate and jiggled it to check its stability. Tony quickly replaced his helmet to hide his expression. Mason thought Tony resembled a villain from a bad eighties science fiction movie with his plastic armor and combat gear. Under other circumstances he would have given Tony a hard time, but not now. He mounted his bike and kicked at the starter.

Running back to his motorcycle, Tony mumbled to himself within his helmet.

"Once more into the breach, dear friends." The phrase both encouraged him and caused him to shutter. Shakespeare never failed to choke him up.

Once they had climbed the grade back to the road, the men engaged their throttles on full. Mason led and Tony followed.

Thirty Five

Lance tugged at his bonds secretly, not wishing to call attention to his actions and alert the girls. Slowly, he moved his wrists apart, testing the tape's strength. He thought he could break through the remainder of the tape with a strong jerk, but if he was wrong, the game was up. If only the girls would leave him alone again, then he could finish chewing through the tape. The thought made his broken tooth throb even more.

"What time is it?" Nikki asked eyeing Lance.

"Seven forty five," Veronica answered, staring through the slats of the shack towards the road. She looked back at Nikki and paced forward a bit. The waiting was taking its toll on Veronica's nerves. She wanted to help the men, to act and play a part in their survival. She felt a touch of that old fear that she had as a little girl, when her father wanted to leave her to help dig survivors from the rubble. No longer a little girl, the woman in her still feared that she might not see Jack and Tony again.

They had passed out of the valley into the trees. The wretched beasts moved in staggered groups, spread out without any sort of organization. They took no note or exception with the many flies that landed on their decaying skin. The large country insects took bite after bite from the cool meat of their carrion. The creatures made no objections. They simply walked. Walked towards something that smelled desirable to what was left of their minds. They could not articulate their desire. The ability to use any sort of language was long gone from the mush that occupied their craniums. They only reacted to the smell. Thoughts no longer occupied their minds, only the urge to feed. Now, driven only by the most primitive of instincts they found a clearing with a building not far from the trees. They did not understand what a building was anymore, only that it smelled appetizing. Like a slug that slithers away from a hot surface, these sickened, slimy creatures, covered with blood and foulness, crawled towards something warm. They slouched and shambled forward towards something to be consumed.

Veronica heard a faint rasp of breathing behind her. For a moment, she thought it was Lance, until he spoke in a frightened tone.

"What was that?" he asked hurriedly.

Veronica's heart seemed to freeze. Lance's voice excited whatever was on the other side of the shack. She heard another dry moan from outside. Something thumped against the wall next to Lance. He bounced forward from the impact. Hands slapped on the walls in greater numbers. Nikki, face blank with terror moved near Veronica in the center of the shack. She pressed her shoulder to Nikki wanting to touch her for reassurance but too afraid to remove her hands from the shotgun.

"They're here!" Nikki almost screamed.

The moans from outside turned to growls, growing louder by the moment. The walls shook but held. Veronica moved to the door to check the two by four that barred it shut. Nikki followed, finding the open room, now free from motorcycles, very large. She stayed close to Veronica out of fear.

The air was thick with the cries of the living dead. Their loud moans seemed to converge closer and closer. Their forms outside blocked the light that penetrated through the small slats, creating horrific, slow moving shadows. Fingernails scrapped and broke off as the beasts tried to claw through the planks. Nikki looked at Veronica with a pale, questioning face. Veronica knew what she was thinking. *How did they get here and what are we going to do*? Veronica took her left hand off the shotgun for a moment and put her finger to her lips, making the gesture for quiet.

Lance decided that now was the time to make a move. The wall behind him shook, throwing him forward with each blow. He thought he could smell the rot coming off their bodies through the wood slats. He threw his arms apart with explosive effort. The tape did not break. He pulled his wrists back up to his mouth and grinded the last bit of tape against his jagged tooth, smashing his nose with his open palms. The pain was excruciating but he did it. The tape separated with the girls too busy to notice. He grabbed the improvised dart and drew the sharpened tip across the tape holding his legs, several times. It perforated the surface of the tape but not all the way through. He sliced at his bonds faster and faster until he freed himself.

Wood crackled and snapped from opposite Lance. On the other side of the wall, something broke through a weak board, about two feet from the floor. The slat separated at a knot hole. A slimy hand forced its way in with the wood bending forward like a saloon door. As a ghoul tried to pull its hand out, skin tore on the rough surface of the wood, clamping down on the thing's wrist. Veronica dashed to the intruder. Nikki stayed put not willing to get close to the greasy claw. Veronica slid the shotgun barrel through the breach in the wall and fired the .410. The creature blew back from the wall leaving a six inch tall, one foot wide gap where its hand had been. She broke open the breach of the shotgun to reload. Lance sprang up, grabbing the open weapon. He punched Veronica hard across the chin. His size and weight advantage over her sent Veronica flying towards Nikki.

"No!" cried Nikki scrambling to point the pistol up towards Lance. Veronica got to her feet and watched Lance pull a green shotgun shell from his pocket. *Where the hell did he get that*? She wondered in anger. He snapped the breach closed and aimed at Veronica. Nikki remembered to flick off the safety and took aim at Lance.

"Put the gun down, little girl or I am going to put a big hole in this bitch's chest," he said.

Nikki was scared. The world was falling apart around her. She wanted to just put the gun down and hope that everything was going to be all right. But she knew it would not be. She knew she could not let Lance have their guns. She pulled back the hammer on the pistol, just like Tony had shown her.

"You have one bullet, I have seven," she said in anger. Her soft voice sounding determined while holding back her panic.

"Yeah, but you're not gonna shoot me. I will shoot her."

"Shoot him Nik," Veronica urged.

The walls shook. A creature looked in the hole next to Lance and growled fiercely; foamy saliva frothing from its chapped and cracked mouth. Lance saw the creature in his peripheral vision but kept his eyes on Veronica. Nikki's heartbeat felt far too fast.

"Give me the shells in your pocket!" Lance demanded.

"Shoot him!" she called to Nikki.

Nikki saw Lance pull back the hammer of the shotgun. She pulled the trigger. She aimed for his chest but the bullet struck Lance in the stomach, just below the sternum. He reeled back in agony. Veronica turned and tried to gain some distance. Lance, still in shock but fueled with rage, tilted the shotgun up as he fell and fired striking Veronica on her left midsection. The shot reverberated through the shack exciting the ghouls even more.

Lance slumped unable to control his legs. He fell to his right against the hole in the wall. A raging creature outside snapped off the four foot plank that was underneath the exposed area. More things came to the breach in the wall. Fingers clawed at Lance. He slapped at their hands impotently with weak defensive swipes. The shotgun slipped from his hands in the struggle. Another plank tore free, lower than the first, exposing more area of the wall. Arms entered the building and seized Lance. He screamed in terror and they answered him with roars of hunger. A two foot by four foot section had now become exposed. A creature poked his head through and sunk its dirty teeth into Lance's forearm. He wailed with a coward's tenor as blood fell in thick drops on the plywood floor.

Nikki watched with her gun still aimed at Lance. She knelt down next to Veronica and saw blood soaking through her motorcycle jersey. Nikki was in a panic. She seemed to vibrate with frustration and fear. Lance screamed causing her attention to shift.

The creatures fought wildly over which one would have access to the hole in the wall. As one ghoul stuck its head into the shack to try and bite Lance, another would pull it out by the shoulders, wanting the meat for themselves. Finally arms began to pull Lance out of the hole. He moved slowly at first, fighting to stay inside. An exposed nail in one of the two by fours dragged a deep crimson gouge across his face as he was pulled along. Merciless jaws assaulted his appendages. Once his head became vulnerable to the outside, the erstwhile Professor Galloway found Lance's face and bit ravenously into his lower lip. Mindy, the former cheerleader slithered her small form through the press of the hungry crowed like a snake and brought her broken and deformed braces down on Lance's neck, silencing his cries.

Nikki watched in horror as Lance's feet disappeared out of the hole. The words, *Oh God, Oh God*, ran over and over in her head. She had never been so scared before in her life. She was alone with those things. They would come in and eat her if she did not do something about it. She had bullets; six in the gun and four in her pocket. *Oh God, Oh God*, the panic replayed. Below her mental mantra of fear, ideas for survival forced themselves to the surface. The thoughts were not words, rather an inspiration. She had to block the hole in the wall before one of the creatures crawled in.

Pocketing the pistol, she ran to the large workbench. With a wide sweep of her arms she cleared every thing off the bench. Paint guns, tools and the red toolbox crashed to the floor with a loud clatter. She kicked the shotgun out of her way, sending it sliding towards Veronica's body. Throwing all of her one hundred and eighteen pounds behind the bench, she was able to bring it to its tipping point. It hung in the air for a moment, balancing on two legs long ways then crashed to the floor. She pushed the bench the way a footballer hits the practice sleds. Slowly it moved towards the gap. The heavy workbench smashed flush with the wall against the two by fours.

Without thinking, Nikki fetched up one of the blow darts and a hammer. She pounded the nail through the bench and into a two by four, smashing the cone. Turning, she pulled the axe off the wall rack and wedged it between the far side of the bench and another two by four on the back wall. The structure was heavy and it just might hold.

She fell to the floor and crawled in utter terror towards Veronica. Nikki did not know what to do. Somewhere in her mind she remembered that blood loss was a bad thing. *What do I use to stop the bleeding?*, she wondered frantically. She saw the little canvas pack that Tony had made for her to use as a pillow the night before. The *Oh God* mantra had silenced.

"He stuffed that with bandages," she whispered.

Thirty Six

The men saw two tattered creatures on the road about a half mile from camp. Mason avoided the first one with a swerve but Tony was not so fortunate. The thing caught him on the helmet with an outstretched arm. Tony was clothes lined off his bike at twenty miles an hour, sending his cycle to the ground five yards away. He landed with a jolt that made him instantly thankful for the protective vest. The creature leaped on Tony, mouth first. It brought its monstrous teeth down onto the shoulder pad of his plastic armor. Tony lifted his heavy helmet and saw the creature trying to bite the plastic. He made a high pitched sound of wonder at his luck. He slipped his hand behind the thing and grabbed its belt, his other underneath the creature's armpit. The gear he wore made his movements more difficult, but he managed to pull with one hand and throw with the other, pushing the frenzied creature off. He rolled to his knees and stood. Tony stomped down with his heavy boot on the creature's head several times, without looking at the result. He had to eliminate the thing as a threat but he did not want to see the gory event. After a few strikes, his foot became unsteady as it slipped about the greasy tissue. Tony turned to see the other creature approach. Mason was behind the thing accelerating his throttle. He stuck out his leg stiffly and sent the ghoul over the side of the road into the unforgiving rocks of the hillside. Mason pulled in close.

"Are you okay?" he yelled over the sound of his engine. Tony nodded in his helmet and walked forward to his bike, scraping the foulness from his boot on the dirt. Lifting the heavy Yamaha, he mounted it, checked the shotgun's barrel for debris and made sure it was secure. Mason glanced at the smashed face of the creature that Tony had dispatched. The distorted remains were thick with horrid pulp. He putted his bike in first gear stopping next to Tony. Mason killed his engine.

"Take off your helmet," Mason said.

Tony removed his helmet and looked questioningly at Mason. He was sweaty but did not appear to be having a crisis, under the circumstances.

"What's up?" Tony asked without a hint of instability.

"I just wanted to see your face, make sure that you're okay."

"Yeah, I am fine," he smiled, "asshole tried to eat my pads."

"You did a number on its head, sure you're okay?" Mason said removing his helmet. He was worried about all the violence his normally peaceful friend was dealing with. This was not practice anymore and Mason wanted to be sure his best friend was all right.

"I tried not to look; just made sure I hit him," Tony said reluctantly.

"Let's coast down in neutral, sneak in quiet." Mason put his helmet back on and dropped his hand on Tony's shoulder pad for encouragement. They engaged the neutral gears with the engines off and let gravity pull them down the hill.

The two motorcycles glided silently into camp. Mason's senses were at full alert. He pulled his bike in front of the truck and leaned it on the bumper. Tony stopped his bike near the picnic bench and tore free the twelve gauge from the handlebars. Looking over the rise he could see what looked like people wandering around the greater camp area. He knew they all were no longer alive by their gait. Dismounting his bike he looked around the camp. The coast was clear. He set his shotgun down and went into his tent. Grabbing a duffel bag of his clothes and setting them on an ice chest, he picked up the chest and carried it to the back of the truck. He knew that the girls would be hungry so he grabbed what he could. Tony picked up his shotgun and threw the pile of Mason's clothes from the table into the truck bed. He looked around to see if there was anything else.

Mason opened the driver's door carefully and popped the hood. The metallic clank of the release sounded very loud in the quiet camp. Something stirred in the brush on the other side of the truck. A low moan was heard as branches started to move. Tony jogged over, switching the shotgun's safety off while he moved. Mason put his hand out to stop him.

"No noise," he whispered as he pulled out his sword. The whisper was not quiet enough. The shattered specter of a man emerged from the foliage. It jerked its rotting head and looked at the men. Mason widened his stance and waited. With a silence shattering growl, it charged. Mason thrust his sword into the oncoming creature's collarbone, sidestepped and directed it to the ground. He stepped on its chest and pulled his sword up, out of the body. It flailed its arms and raged louder. Mason lifted his sword high and drove the steel chisel tip into the thing's right eye. The *Katana* blade broke through bone, cleaving its putrid grey matter. Mason pulled his sword free and wiped the tip off on the creature's shirt.

Tony began to hook up the jumper cables. Leaving the battery in the milk crate, he attached the cables to the proper poles. He ran around and jumped into the truck, placing the shotgun back on safety and laying it next to him. He slammed the glove box closed and removed the keys. Placing the keys in the ignition, he turned them. The engine cycled weakly then caught. The truck started.

Tony looked out the window; the dead were attracted to the sound of the engine. Mason pulled his bike out from in front of the truck while stuffing the jumper cables back into the milk crate. Looking back towards the truck, Mason froze. Tony removed his helmet and stuck his head out the window. What he saw horrified him. He now knew what had given Mason such pause.

A male child came crawling up the hill into their camp. It topped the grade and now looked at Mason. The boy's chest looked like it had been scrapped away with a wood rasp. Dried dark ooze congealed over the remnants of its torn pajamas. The little creature just stared at the motionless Mason. Tony pulled the shotgun up and extended it out the window to his friend. The creatures from the campground were drawing close, but Jack did not seem to notice.

"Kill it dude," Tony said offering the gun. Mason looked at his *Katana* for a moment then drove the blade in the ground. The sword stood straight up, seeming to vibrate. He moved the three steps it took to reach the truck, never taking his eyes of the child. Mason did not blink though his eyes began to water. The bloody creature growled at his movement. Deciding that the man before him was food, the boy let out a nasally pigs wail and began running.

In one motion, Mason spun the shotgun around, clicked off the safety and fired. Six high velocity steel pellets spread out in a tight pattern from the barrel, turning the oncoming boy's tiny head into a thick dark mist. The body ran headless for two more steps, then collapsed. Mason looked away, into the sky, and cried out. The boy was too much. *A kid, a child, turned into one of those things. Something so innocent transformed into a monster.* He hurt for the boy in a way that he could not feel for an adult. He was angry that he had to destroy the creature, even though he knew he was right to do so. Mason turned and punched an angry dent into the side of his truck.

The dead drew closer. One shirtless ghoul made its way down the dirt path to camp. Mason pumped a fresh round into the shotgun and fired, blowing it back several feet. He handed the shotgun back through the window. Tony pumped the shotgun and took aim at an approaching corpse. He fired and hit it in the shoulder from ten yards. It spun around and fell. Mason walked to the back of the truck.

"We have to get out of here!" Tony yelled, pulling three shotgun shells from his pocket. *What the hell is Jack doing*? Tony wondered. He fed the shells into the bottom of the weapon one at a time. Opening the door he stood up, leaning out of the truck, to see around the camp. Mason returned with a sleeping bag and spread it over the body of the boy, covering him completely. Tony could see a ghoul shambling in the trees to his right. He aimed over the cab of the truck and fired, caving in its forehead.

Mason said a quick prayer for the boy. He retrieved his sword from the ground, replaced it in the scabbard on his handlebars and mounted the bike.

"Let's get the hell out of here," Mason said to Tony, then kicked his starter. The two men pulled their vehicles out of camp, followed by many bedraggled ghouls.

Thirty Seven

The pounding and shaking of the shack had been replaced with the wet echoes of tearing flesh. Muffled moans and cries sounded through the full mouths of the undead. Nikki tried to push the loud slurps and chewing out of her mind. She unraveled a package of bandages and pulled up Veronica's shirt. On the left side there was an eggplant shaped bruise. The center of the wound had a little blood yet it appeared more like a deep scrape. Nikki expected a large bloody mess. Knowing nothing about the type of wounds a shotgun makes, she pressed the thick gauze to the injury.

Veronica felt the pressure in her half conscious state. Through the miasma of pain and shock that clouded her senses, she forced herself awake.

"What happened?" she asked opening her eyes. A frantic Nikki put her finger to her mouth in a shush gesture. She was shaking with panic but was trying to bandage Veronica's wound. *Why am I alive?* Veronica asked herself. Putting a hand to her side she felt that she was intact. The injury stung like hell but was not bleeding. *Stings like hell?* She lifted her head and had to stop herself from laughing.

"Rock salt," she whispered. She lay back for a moment and listened. The noises seemed to come from the far corner of the shack.

There was no more pounding, just the sickening sounds of an ungodly feast. Bending up to a sitting position was out of the question, the pain was far too intense. She rolled over, got to her knees, and rose up with Nikki's aid. Looking at the corner she saw the overturned bench that Nikki used as a makeshift reinforcement. Lance was gone. Grunts and growls of rage caused Veronica's imagination to assume that there was some fighting going on over food. The things were fighting over his body. Nikki drew the pistol from her pocket, looked at Veronica and pointed to the corner. Veronica understood. The undead were busy eating, when they were done, they would want more.

Nikki remembered what Tony had told her about the pistol. To keep a running count in reverse of how many bullets she had left. The gun was fully loaded, she had fired once. That left six bullets, one in the chamber and five in the clip. There were four more, rounds, as he called them, in the extra clip in her pocket. She had fired the gun at Lance but shot to low. Tony said that could happen, that she should correct for that the next time she shoots. Her fear had gone away just a little. She was not frozen in place now, she had a fighting chance and she was going to take it. The horrible feasting sounds began to die down. The quiet gave her hope that the things might be satisfied. The way her luck was going, she knew that she had to be ready to fend off an attack. Veronica seemed fine. Bruised and scraped up, but she was alive, bringing such an incredible relief to Nikki.

A dull thud hit the wall. Veronica leaned over and picked up the .410 shotgun from the floor, ignoring the pain in her midsection. She pulled two shells from her pocket, inserted one, and palmed the other. She checked the watch. It read ten minutes after eight; help was a long way off.

Thirty Eight

Mason flew up the uneven mountain roads. He was moving a lot faster without a passenger. Tony followed making better time in the truck. He was more confident driving a vehicle as opposed to a motorcycle. The Chevy's modified engine and well made suspension handled the grade with ease. They had left the growing number of ghouls converging on their camp far behind now. All they had to do was collect the girls and the spoiled hillbilly and they could be off. Things were looking up.

The pounding resumed, growing more intense by the moment. *The creatures must be able to smell us*, Veronica thought. Then it occurred to her, *what if the men do not make it back*? Cold sweat ran down the back of her neck. Veronica could not allow herself to think that way, she had to do something. Looking around the room she saw various tools sprawled across the floor in the opposite corner. She knew the bench would not hold if enough of the creatures concentrated their efforts there. Veronica wondered how many there were. The pounding was spread out now, surrounding the shack from all sides. They would have to fight the things off until there were no more or help arrived. She bent to Nikki's ear and spoke as low as she could.

"We have to fight them off. Shoot for the head. When you are out of bullets, use the shovels, the pick, anything you can," she whispered. Nikki looked at her with brokenhearted fear, but somehow, she nodded. The pounding continued.

Behind the tool rack, underneath the hanging shovels, a four foot plank creaked as a female creature's small fingers found purchase through the slats. Veronica heard the squeaks as old nails were pulled slowly from the two by fours. The space grew as disgustingly thin fingers wormed in. They pulled to the tune of mounting moans. The plank gave way, its master falling in a sudden shift of momentum. A four foot wide opening had formed in the single plank's absence. The missing board was too low for a good shot. They only saw the chests and shoulders of three creatures. Veronica raised her weapon. Nikki nervously brought the pistol up and pulled back the hammer.

"Wait, let me," Veronica said with authority, pulling her own hammer back. She was afraid that both she and Nikki would shoot at the same monster and waste precious bullets. Finally, a creature bent its head down and reached in. Veronica took a step, not wanting to accidentally hit the wall and make the space any larger. She aimed the shotgun just eight inches from the creature's pruned face and fired. Three small nails and two bolts were driven by the expanding gasses generated in the gun, into the creature's temple. He fell back, his arm sliding out of the hole like a retreating eel. Veronica backed away a step and opened the shotgun. Another creature shoved its distorted jaws into the break in the wall, growling, trying to bite at the air. Veronica removed the spent shell and placed another in the gun, snapping the breach closed. Nikki moved in front of her and took aim. The small pistol barked a loud pop as Nikki's shoulders jolted with a sudden flinch. Blood erupted from the creature's ears as the invading bullet created massive overpressure within its skull. The thing fell.

"Five left and four in my pocket," said the small blonde with determination. A large ghoul came into view. He was muscular and tall but through the hole, all Nikki could see was his broad chest and the filthy shirt he wore that read, "Paul Frank". Bruised and bloody hands ripped free the plank above the hole making it taller. Nikki saw his damaged face. She recognized him from an English class at the JC. He was covered with what looked like deep burns but the flat top hair style was unmistakable.

"Clark?" Nikki asked stunned. Veronica saw her hesitation.

"I know him," Nikki mumbled.

Veronica moved closer, shotgun raised and put a tight pattern of scrap metal into Clark's left eye. The back of his head erupted clumps of foul gruel.

"Knew him," Veronica said while replacing the shotgun shell. She put her hand on Nikki's shoulder. "He is not a he anymore."

Nikki looked shocked. She had a crush on Clark once. He was the best baseball player in her high school. Two more creatures broke her spell of remembrance as they moved enraged with hunger in front of the hole.

"You take left, I'll take the right," Veronica said aiming. They both fired. At the range they were shooting, they had hit everything they shot at until now. Nikki, still shaken from seeing the reanimated corpse of someone she knew, missed her target completely. She stomped her foot in anger and concentrated. Another pop from her pistol and the creature was gone. Nikki was upset about missing but she resolved to try harder when aiming. Trying to remember how many bullets she had now, she realized that she had forgotten. Five then one miss and one hit. *Okay*, Nikki thought, *three in the gun and four in my pocket.*

Reloading, Veronica thought that things might be alright if the creatures keep lining up for them to shoot. The monsters did not seem to exhibit any sort of organization or understanding. If the building could hold, they just might make it. As if to spoil her hopes, a powerful jolt rocked the bench at the other side of the room. It pushed in a few inches from the bottom, arms projecting through the gap it made.

"Watch this side, aim for the head!" Veronica yelled pointing to the hole. She ran for the bench and pushed it back towards the wall, leaning her weight to hold it in place. The effort caused her a screaming pain in her bruised flank but she fought through it.

Nikki carefully put a round through the forehead of an elderly looking male ghoul. She desperately wanted more bullets. She reminded herself that after one more bullet she could switch to the clip in her pocket, giving her four plus one in the chamber. Counting the rounds strengthened her resolve during the crisis but the dwindling number of bullets began to worry her.

Veronica scanned the room. Staying on the floor with her back to the bench was not the best use of her time. Nikki was going to need her help. Seeing the pickaxe, she had an idea.

"Throw me the pick!" She yelled over the sounds of the attacking throng. Nikki had never seen a pickaxe before, and her expression showed it.

"The big one that looks like a pointy axe," Veronica said nodding to the rack.

Nikki understood, but it would mean that she had to get close to the hole in the wall next to the pick. She moved in and stretched her arm as far as it could go. Grabbing the handle from the tool rack, a short ghoul popped up in the space and growled. Nikki fired her weapon in surprise and hit it in the hand, dropping her hold on the pick.

"Shit!" Nikki said taking aim with both hands. She fired, collapsing the creature. Grasping the handle of the pickaxe, she lifted it off the rack. The pick was heavy in her hand. She controlled its descent and tossed it towards Veronica. It skidded across the floor, stopping a foot away. Veronica stretched her foot out and snagged the top of the pickaxe. She flexed her leg, the contracting muscles doubling the pain in her abdomen. It dragged slowly towards her, enough that she could reach with her hand. Her next move would be risky but there was no choice. She placed the shotgun on the floor and slid it a couple of feet away. Forgetting her pain, she bolted up with the pick allowing the bench to slide forward a foot under the pressure of the invading monsters. She kicked the bench hard, flushing it against the studs of the wall. Bringing the pickaxe high over her head, Veronica slammed the sharp end into and through the plywood floor very close to the bench. The pick's head locked the bench to the wall solidly. The more the beasts pushed, the stronger it held. Veronica retrieved her shotgun, staring at her work. It was indeed secure.

Nikki stepped back from the rack, ejected the magazine from the spent weapon, and fished the last clip from her pocket. She slammed the magazine home and closed the action, in the manner that she was taught just twelve hours earlier. Two more creatures came to the breach in the wall. Their heads were not visible, just arms shooting forward into the shack. *Why can't I see their heads?* Nikki wondered. With only four bullets left, her only hope was to wait for a better shot.

Outside of the shack, the fallen undead had formed into a pile of once human remains. The more Nikki dispatched, the higher the stack of bodies beneath the breach grew.

The walking dead had neither respect nor reason to regard their fallen brethren. They stood upon the slippery remains of the others, clawing for access to the warm living matter within the shack. Arms outstretched, they did not need to see their prey; their instincts told them where the meat was. The former cheerleader, Mindy had taken a good bite out of Lance because she was small. She was able to wriggle in between the larger creatures. Once the feeding frenzy began, she was tossed aside by the hungry aggression of the others. Her braces, torn from such animal like biting had come undone in several places. The wires now protruded through the decayed tissue of her swollen black lips. As the others slipped about on top of puss filled wrecks of inhuman creatures, she found herself forcing her fingers through a different part of the shack. There was food inside and her instincts wanted it. Hunger and rage blended forming a hellish alchemy. As slivers of old weathered pine slipped underneath the skin of her fingers, they curled around the plank and pulled. She formed thunderous cries from the constricted passageways of her throat as the plank flexed outward. Wordless desire formed in the gelatinous stew that made up her brain, the urge to consume hot flesh. The plank flexed further. Wood stressed from the middle but the nails on each side resisted.

Much to Nikki's relief, Veronica rejoined her side, shotgun at the ready. They still could not see the heads of the creatures through the breach. Veronica thought against trying to poke the thin barrel of her weapon out the hole to try for a head shot. The arms of the beasts could find her, or she might loose her gun to their grasp.

"Grab that shovel," she said to Nikki.

Nikki did not hear her over the continuous thumping on the walls. She just stood, pistol raised, sweaty and visibly shaken. Her eyes trained on the creatures waiting for a good target. There was a dark determination on her countenance that Veronica never expected to see. She did not bother asking Nikki again. Veronica laid the shotgun down next to her feet, being reminded of her pain once again as she stooped. She picked up the longer of the two shovels and stood. Holding the shovel, she thrust at the swiping hands. Moving to the side, she jabbed in between a pair of outstretched arms. The sharp tip of the spade dug a small gouge in the ribs of a ghoul. She thrust again and sliced at the thing's right armpit. Veronica pushed forward, forcing its shoulder away from the breach. She ducked to avoid its other flailing appendage. It grabbed her shovel and pulled it from her hands out through the hole. As the monster tore the shovel away, it bent down for a moment allowing Nikki a shot. She fired with one eye closed, determined not to waste any more bullets. A copper coated chunk of lead sailed into its cheek and out the top of its head. It rolled back and fell, still clutching the shovel.

"Three left," Nikki said with her gun still pointing at the opening. Her hands shook as she concentrated on her aim.

In the corner opposite the bench, on the same wall as the hole that Nikki was watching, a plank violently broke in the center. Veronica, alerted by the sound of creaking wood, snapped up her shotgun and aimed at the girl creature with the distorted mouth. Another larger ghoul threw the cheerleader easily aside to gain access. It lowered its face in towards the gap and received a blast from Veronica's shotgun. Homemade shrapnel shredded the beast's rotting features.

How many more are out there, wondered Veronica. She replaced a shotgun shell feeling only two more left in her pocket. The hammering of fists and palms on the walls told here that there were plenty more monsters to deal with. She wanted to save her shots. Nikki fired again, the loud report making Veronica flinch.

"Did you hit him?" Veronica yelled.

"Two bullets left," was her only answer.

Two corpses appeared in front of Veronica, furiously tearing at the slats. More planks tore off, making her breach a foot and a half by four feet. Only one column of four foot planks stood firm between the two breaches. The framing of the shack was durable however, a broken plank left a space where the creatures could get their hands in, and tear larger openings. Veronica wanted to know what time it was, but had no time to check her watch. She hefted the shotgun to her cheek and fired. A creature went down with a wet sound. She reloaded the shotgun.

Nikki was trying not to hyperventilate. She was concentrating with all her faculties on her opening. Her consciousness had formed into a sort of tunnel vision. She knew that she had two bullets left. She had to hit her targets. She had missed twice and was not going to miss again. A mop of brown hair appeared in her breach. The creature was female, in a cheerleading shirt. As Nikki looked at the girl beast, her rapid heartbeat skipped its rhythm. The creature was familiar. Nikki knew her from school. *Knew her*, Nikki thought, *past tense*. The creature growled a disgusting display of torn braces. Nikki fired. The .380 hit the young monster in the temple, blasting out her ear on the other side. Nikki hit her target and became very distressed; she only had one bullet left.

"Last bullet!" Nikki hollered.

Veronica lifted her weapon, pushed it in close through the swinging arms of a creature and fired. The thing went down, blown away from the shack by the blast. Reloading her weapon, Veronica felt like she was part of an assembly line of death. The constant thumping and clawing at the building was much less now, but still encompassed the shack. They were very fortunate that the creatures had not concentrated on the breaches. *These things are not very smart*, she thought. She had an idea. Veronica backed away to the other side of the shack. She kept her eye on the breach but moved very close to the far wall. Two ghouls were there hammering and yowling for entrance. She could see the shadows of their forms through the slats.

"Hey guys. Are you hungry? I am right here!" she yelled in a wavering voice.

She slapped her hand on the wall repeatedly. Their response was a horrifying increase in pounding. Their snarls and howls became even more ferocious. Her goal to encourage the ghouls on the other side in the hopes of keeping them there was successful. It also had the effect of exciting the others. A creature that had been pressing against the door for sometime, decided to try another area. It rounded the corner to Nikki's breach, put a foul claw on the top of the lower plank, and lost its footing on the slippery mass of bodies, tearing the wood free as it fell. The plank flew off like a shingle blown away in a storm. The breach was growing. The creature braced itself on the pile of bodies and attempted to push up. Nikki fired; her slug punched a hole into the top of the thing's head, exiting just under the chin. The corpse fell as if it were suddenly switched off. Flies soon found the body and started their work.

The pistol stopped with the slide locked back, chamber open. It was empty. There were no more bullets. Nikki was spent. She stood, looking at the weapon; at her hopes for survival. The incessant pounding and moans of hunger had diminished since the siege began, yet Nikki could not tell the difference. It took Nikki a moment to realize that Veronica was yelling at her.

"We got to keep them on this side, away from the holes," Veronica's voice said from afar. Nikki turned and saw what her friend was doing. Fear welled up within the young blonde with the understanding of Veronica's plan. She moved to the far side filled with disgust. Nikki did not want to get close to the walls. She began to slap on the planks while her stomach turned from the foul smell of their putrescence.

"Keep them on this side," Veronica urged. Nikki pounded harder. The plan was sound. She slid the pistol into her pocket and used both hands, making sure to keep a two by four in front of her, thinking that it was the strongest part of the wall. Veronica left to attend the breaches. From the center of the shack, she tried to count the creatures. There were two on Nikki's wall, two shadows at the back, possibly three. She saw one shadow move towards the breach wall and aimed her weapon in response. It appeared through the corner of the break as Veronica fired. The shot shell tore away the skin on the thing's forehead and imploded its left eye, though it only reeled back. The home made shell failed to penetrate the hard bone. It recovered its balance and reached into the shack, roaring with hunger. Quickly reloading, her fingers were like jelly, but they managed to function. Veronica snapped the gun closed and took careful aim. She fired, tearing away the top of the monster's forehead.

That was it. No more ammunition and four, possibly more things to deal with. She looked to Nikki.

"Keep them on that side," Veronica said

Nikki's fear calmed a little as she pounded; the physical act forming some sort of release valve. She felt like venting, letting her anger out.

"Come on you bastards, over here, its hot and delicious!" Nikki screamed with fury.

Her words sent a shiver down Veronica's spine. The thought of being hot and delicious was not very comforting. Veronica knelt feeling her side throb and set down the shotgun. She quickly pulled the two paint guns towards her. Leaning out her long body, she retrieved the last shovel, a machete and a hammer. She pulled her haul close to Nikki and left it strewn about the floor at her feet.

"Come on you fuckers, I am right her," Nikki continued, with tears in her eyes. Her anger fueled by the stink of the creatures' rotting proximity drove her outbursts. Veronica handed her the shovel. Nikki accepted it and continued her pounding. Picking up one of the paint guns, Veronica made sure that it was ready to fire. She had no idea if the dart gun would work, but it did fire something. Anything was worth a try now. Jack said that she would have to be close. The gun was tuned to fire at full strength. She would aim for the eyes. If the dart failed to make it through the orbital bone, at least she would be able to blind another creature. Thinking that she might need two shots, Veronica knelt down and put the strap of the second paint gun over her shoulder. She stood. There were no targets at the moment.

"You mother fuckers, come on, you know you want this!" Nikki screamed at the creatures through the slats. She was practically crying but her words said rage. Veronica put her hand to her shoulder. Nikki flinched back in fear, startled by her touch.

"Take it easy," Veronica said. Nikki looked at her with the tormented eyes of someone on the edge of madness. Sweat and dust clung to her face while her lower lip trembled. Veronica put her arms around Nikki and felt her go weak. The young girl whimpered. In the relative peace provided by the reduced numbers of attackers, she whispered reassurance to Nikki.

"There are very few left, we are going to make it." Nikki pulled away and stood straight up. For the first time she noticed that the thumping was much less now. Her own pounding and screaming had been too loud for her to recognize the difference. Reality seemed clearer to Nikki, maybe they were going to get through this. Veronica removed a rubber band from her pocket. Adjusting the strap of the paint gun over her other shoulder, she tied her hair back.

"The shooting gallery is over, now we have to fight," Veronica said trying to encourage her friend. Nikki nodded and started pounding again, this time with more control.

"Hey guys, I am still here, come on," she looked to Veronica with a touch of confidence. They followed her voice from the outside with pitiful starved moans.

Veronica crept slowly towards the second breach. Two shadows of the undead signaled that they were on the other side of its corner. She thought about luring one over to the breach to try the darts, but feared the other following it. She was willing to attempt using the air rifle against one creature, not two. It would be best to deal with the things one at a time. Looking on the floor she saw the machete. A horrid idea formed in her mind.

"Keep it up, its working," she said to Nikki as she put down both dart guns. Snapping up the machete and a hammer she went to the corner of the shack opposite the breach. The two creatures were on the outside clawing and pushing against the pine planks. Veronica stooped and looked at the form furthest from the breach. It was thin and small, possibly female. Sizing up the creature with her knowledge of anatomy, she found the area between the boards that would work best.

"Hey there, who's hungry," she said through the planks. The creatures pressed harder, dragging jagged fingernails on the wall in a starving frenzy.

Veronica braced both hands on the handle of the machete and placed the tip in the small space between the planks. She ran the blade into the creature's rib cage with all her strength. At first the tip met with resistance, pushing against tough tissue. Then as the blade cut into skin, muscle, and soft viscera, the machete slid further. Foul gas escaped from the opening in the thing's flesh with a slow wet whoosh. It was gristly work that turned her stomach, but it had to be done. Pounding on the handle with the hammer, she forced the blade as far as possible into the creature. As long as it did not push away from the wall, it should stay in place.

Now the hard part, Veronica thought. She dropped the hammer and scooped up the paint guns. Looking at the corner directly beside her breach, she saw the other ghoul's shape. Luring the thing over frightened her but once again, it had to be done. Veronica forced herself to get very close to the opening.

"Hey you over there," she called. The ghoul stopped pounding.

"Over here," she said again.

It moved fast, almost feeling its way around the corner. Veronica raised the paint gun, aiming for its eye. She fired. The dart was propelled by a large burst of compressed gas. It glided through the jelly of the eye, penetrated the orbital bone and lodged without harming the brain. The ghoul roared and sought after Veronica's flesh with festering arms.

"Shit!" she cursed, dropping the paint gun and readying the other. She moved in close, extending the gun as far away from her body as possible and fired. Jack's gun was the more powerful of the two. It coughed a four inch dart at over three hundred feet per second through the thing's eye and into its brain. Amazed that her plan had worked, Veronica looked on the floor for another dart.

Nikki's voice was growing horse. Tired of yelling, she had been able to keep her ghouls interested by prodding the wall here and there with the shovel. Seeing Veronica successfully dealing with the remaining creatures increased her optimism for their survival. She watched Veronica remove the barrel and load another dart in a paint gun.

"What time is it?" Nikki asked with a scratchy voice.

"Eight fifty," Veronica said looking up from Jack's watch disappointed.

Looking around the room at the various tools, Veronica was out of ideas. There were at least three more creatures out there. The machete appeared to be holding the one ghoul at the rear, but the others were free. She was not sure about using the darts again. Veronica wanted other options.

"Do you have any ideas?" she asked Nikki.

Nikki thought and looked at the workbench. She had an idea but was afraid to mention it.

"We could move the bench away and smash their heads," Nikki said.

"What?" Veronica questioned in disbelief.

"Look how low the hole is. Get them to try and crawl in, then you smash their heads."

Veronica looked at the bench. It was very low, about two feet from floor to the top of the hole. The things would have to bend down to gain entrance. They would make perfect targets at that level, crawling in head first. She was optimistic that they could pull it off with only one creature, but two of the bastards made her nervous. Still, the thought of the men not making it back, frightened her. She had to work under the assumption that there was no help coming. Looking at the axe, she thought it might be the perfect weapon for the job. If they managed to kill one monster, its body would block the hole, making it more difficult for the other to get in. As the second one struggled over the remains, she could use the axe again. *It could work*, Veronica thought. She took a deep breath.

"Okay, you pull the pick out and I will…" Veronica stopped and listened. She heard the distinct sound of a motorcycle wining high in the distance. Both women exhaled in exhaustion and looked at each other with relief.

Thirty Nine

Topping the rise onto the flat open area at high speed, Mason saw the shack in the distance. Something was different, something was wrong; something was trying to break in. He cranked his throttle down hard and flew across the dirt road. A few moments later, Tony appeared in the truck. Mason's approach alerted the ghouls. Tony bounced the truck across the field honking the horn. They turned and started towards Mason. He stopped his bike twenty feet from the shack and laid it on the ground. Pulling his *Katana* from the scabbard, he squared off with the two creatures, sword ready. Mason swung his sword hard at a male ghoul, striking it in the neck. The blade severed the vertebrae, yet lodged deep in the tough muscles. The corpse dropped, its head leaning grotesquely to one side. Mason pulled away from the monster as it fell allowing the sharp blade to carve itself free. The second creature lunged at him. Mason ducked low, bringing his shoulder pad into the thing's midsection. Mason exerted an explosive leap from his legs, propelling the ghoul up and over his shoulder, to land flat on its back. It floundered on the ground, arms flailing.

"Haven't done that in a while," he said thinking of his football days. Tony parked the truck next to Mason and emerged with the twelve gauge.

"Take care of this one," Mason said sprinting towards the shack. Tony took aim at the creature as it rolled over. He fired, tilling the ghoul's brain into the soil.

"Veronica, are you guys all right?" he yelled knocking on the door. He heard the two by four being removed. He opened the door.

Veronica stood holding an axe, Nikki, held a shovel. They stood ready with looks of exhausted courage. Jack removed his helmet and let it drop to the ground. Veronica's face softened as she smiled. She approached Jack while letting her axe drag and drop to the floor. Emerging outside, she threw her arms around him. He held her, wishing that he was not wearing so much padding and gear. Looking over her shoulder, he now saw the extent of the damage on the back wall of the shack. Nikki dropped her shovel and sat down in the middle of the room. Tony ran to the door.

"There is one more at the back, stuck to the wall," Veronica said to Tony over Jack's shoulder. She closed her eyes as Tony ran to deal with the creature. She breathed the fresh air in and out slowly, savoring the moment.

Tony found the last creature on the far side wall. It raged at his presence. The creature was a female who had lost much of her looks. Puss dripped from the machete as it pushed itself off the wall to gain access to Tony. As it slid its foul frame free of the rusty blade, Tony took aim, this time, with his eyes open.

"Clear!" he shouted and fired.

Within the shack, the blast from Tony's shotgun made Nikki jump. She started to cry. Veronica let go of Jack to attend her friend.

"We are going to need a minute," she whispered. Jack nodded and pushed the door closed.

Walking out in front of the shack, he saw Tony looking at something. Jack joined him. Lying on the ground was the badly eaten upper torso of Lance Richardson. There were no legs, just a trail of thick blood that diminished some three feet from his chest, where a pair of filthy shorts and bones lay. The only way they recognized the man was his bloody but still discernibly blond hair. The face muscles were almost gone, just a greasy red skull underneath his frosted coif. Bits of tough tendon shined grayish reflections like fish scales covered with foul gruel.

"What happened? I mean, where did they come from?" Tony asked.

"I don't know," Jack said low, "But those girls went through some shit."

Inside the shack, Veronica was kneeling, holding Nikki in her arms, rocking her back and forth gently.

"It's okay Nik, let it out." Veronica had tears of her own in her eyes. She reassured Nikki and herself at the same time.

"It is over," she said in a whisper. Holding Nikki for a while longer, the terror and stress of the day surrendered to peace. They had survived the hellish conflict.

"I am never going to be the same again" Nikki said low in her injured voice.

"No, but you will be stronger," Veronica said missing her father.

When Nikki was ready, Veronica helped her to stand.

Forty

Jack drove while the others slept. Veronica was next to him; next to her were Nikki, and finally Tony. Jack's motorcycle was secured by tie downs in the back, swaying gently as the truck negotiated the dirt road. It was over now, yet Jack was disappointed in himself for leaving the women alone at the shack. It would have been much safer to have brought them along on the motorcycles. *Hindsight and all that crap*, he thought. He was relieved to have the gang all together. *We got away with it*, he thought.

Up ahead in the distance, he saw the unmistakable grey tones of a paved road; civilization would not be far. As the wheels of his Chevy transitioned to asphalt he relaxed and cracked his window open a little for some fresh air. The loud squeaks and creaks of his old truck settled down with the smooth surface. He looked over his sleeping companions. He gazed at Veronica. She had let her hair down when Jack put his bike in the back of the truck. He thought it looked nice that way. *Even without a shower for two days, she looks pretty damn good.* Moving his eyes back to the road he saw that the sun was beginning to set.

They had stopped for a break at noon; spending three hours talking and cleaning up a little with melted water from the ice chest. Thinking back on how long he had been driving, he realized that it was very fortunate that they went back for the truck. It would have taken him two days to walk over this range. After seeing how the women handled themselves at the shack, he had no doubt that would have survived the hike. But it would have taken quite a while. He wondered what time it was. He looked back to Veronica. She was still wearing his watch. Carefully, he put his fingers around her wrist to see the watch face. She turned her head to him without opening her eyes.

"What are you doing?" she inquired softly. He did not anticipate such awareness from her. To hide his surprise his quick mind formed a joke.

"Just trying to get a little action," he said deadpan with straight face.

"What?" she whispered while opening her eyes in disbelief.

"I wanted to see what time it is," he said smiling.

He let go of her wrist to concentrate on the road. She yawned something like "Oh," and looked at the watch.

"Eight thirty three," she said stretching her tired neck.

Looking out the window she saw the pleasant green surroundings.

"How much further?" she asked.

"Not long now, we are on pavement, we should start to see the town soon," he said.

"Roll the window down some more, its stuffy in here," she yawned.

"Well it doesn't help that you had beans for dinner last night," he said with a smile. With all the terror behind them, Jack was glad to express his humorous side. Surprised by his quip, Veronica laughed and punched him affectionately on the shoulder.

"Shut up" she said playfully. It felt good to laugh. She found herself relieved that after everything they had been through, she could still smile.

Jack cranked the handle allowing cool air to enter the cab. There was a faint smell of a smoke on the wind. As he drove it grew stronger. He thought about the burning car at the campground and wondered if it had started a fire on the other side of the mountain.

"Is that a fire?" Veronica asked smelling the smoke.

"It smells like one."

The road inclined gently downwards. Soon, the left side of the hills receded away into a vast open plane. Emerging onto a long stretch of road that traversed the mountain, Jack guessed that they were around fifteen hundred feet up. Not long now indeed. Farmland dominated the view to their left but no town. The open sky was hazy. The setting sun stretched in to a beautiful pattern of orange and burnt sienna.

"Why have we not run out of gas yet?" Veronica asked, feeling a desire to talk.

"Saddle tanks," Jack said pointing to a switch on his console, "I have two twenty gallon tanks, one on each side."

"That is convenient," she mumbled, leaning her weary head on his shoulder. Jack did not mind at all.

"Yeah, until you have to fill it."

"So, what do you want for dinner?" she asked drowsily.

"Surprise me," he said. She closed her eyes and just leaned on him.

They continued like that for some time, driving downwards. The smell of smoke increased.

"It's getting worse," Veronica said lifting her head. Tony roused and stretched his legs as best he could in his seat. He smelled the fire as well. Rounding a wide corner to the right, the sun in its final moments on its journey to the west, they saw the source of the smoke. Mason stopped the truck, waking Nikki with the shift in momentum. She jerked forward and righted herself in a tense stiffness, frightened from the abrupt awakening.

"What's going on?" she asked almost desperate.

The others could not answer. Parts of the town below were on fire. They were too far up to discern individuals in the streets, but the lack of fire fighting equipment and the various unchecked blazes told them that the dead had come to the town.

"Oh my God," Nikki said bending forward to look out the wind shield. Mason let off the break and started the truck rolling forward slowly. He reached down and turned on the radio. Rotating the dial, he found a station.

"…this weekend of terror across the globe. Scientists at the CERN observatory in France have named the meteor shower Cerberus. The first reports of contamination came in late Saturday night. Many believe that the phenomenon started as early as Thursday, July tenth, yet went unreported because of their unbelievable nature. Many major metropolitan areas have been overrun by this epidemic. New York, Chicago, Dallas and Los Angeles have been hard hit. One area with very little contact is San Francisco. Officials with the neighboring city of Oakland have barricaded the entrances and exits of the Bay Bridge. Oakland citizens including some disreputable criminal elements are working side by side with the police to make a stand against these, for lack of a better word, Zombies… "

As they drove further down, the radio continued with reports of growing global violence.

Nikki gazed out over her hometown fearful for her parent's safety.

"We are going to need more bullets," Nikki said in a quiet but determined voice.

"Where is this ammunition plant you were talking about?" Mason asked.

Nikki pointed to a building in the distance…

Learn more about the author at www.myspace.com/solis70

Hadrian Publishing

Recommends for your further enjoyment...

RISE AND WALK: Pathogen

The terror continues as the numbers of the undead increase.

Available in mid 2007 from Hadrianpublishing.com

Also, please have a look at our friends...

Hard Up to English

A comedic social commentary about dating, love, relationships and, aging singles. Written by Emily Ruiz. Available at Authorhouse.com

David Moody Author of the AUTUMN series.

www.infectedbooks.co.uk

The Best Horror T-Shirts and Collectables on the Web

www.Rottencotton.com

Dastardly Studios, Digital creativity at it's best.

www.DastardlyStudios.com

Talented writers on the web...

Cassandra Lee

http://cassandraleehorror.bravehost.com/

Printed in the United States
83573LV00006B/50/A